NO FAIRYTALE

A short story collection

By Sylva Fae

Copyright

All rights reserved. No part of this book may be reproduced or distributed in any form without prior written permission from the author, with the exception of non-commercial uses permitted by copyright law.

Cover created by Sharon Brownlie of Aspire Book Covers:

https://aspirebookcovers.com/

Proof reading by Kay Lynne Booth and Melanie P Smith – thank you both.

All interior images are from Deposit Photos.

Dedication

Special thanks to Geraldine McIntyre, Christine Southworth, Stuart Weyman and Matt Martin, the dedicated admin team of Mindful Monsters and friends.

Thanks also to the rest of my Mindful Monster friends. Please head straight to the Naughty Step!

Foreword

This is a very random collection of short stories, some of which have appeared previously in online publications and anthologies. I love creating children's books, but I always relish the opportunity to write adult stories. Short stories fulfil my need to break out of the children's author mould, and dabble in a variety of genres. In this collection, you will find everything from simple feel-good tales, to supernatural, crime, fantasy, sci-fi, comedy, adventure, suspense, and horror.

I love to read novels, but occasionally, the time constraints enforced by a busy family life mean that a quick short story has to satisfy my need to read. With this in mind, the stories are grouped into three categories: long shorts, short shorts and flash fiction. I've added the average read times to the index to help you choose a story to fit the time you have available.

All good fiction starts with a basis in truth. Writers have a habit of people-watching, observing life as inspiration for their next book. I am guilty of this, and as such, most of the characters and scenarios come from my own experiences, or those I've observed. Can you spot the real places and characters in the book?

Index

Long Shorts	Reading time	Page
Switchback	15m	1
Murky Windows	26m	18
Earworm	14m	42
A Magic Box of Apples	21m	55
Hollin Hey	11m	74
Lilies for the Mantel	10m	85
Penitence	15m	94
Vanished	35m	107

Short Shorts		
No Fairytale	5m	139
The Ring	4m	144
The Christmas Box	5m	150
Red Lights	3m	157
Scarlett and the Wolf	5m	159
The Witch	4m	164
Secret Santa	4m	169
The Pitch	5m	174
The Cupcake Hustle	7m	180
Dwelling in the Shadows	8m	186

Flash Fiction	Reading time	Page
For Sale	1.5m	193
Cake Roulette	2m	195
Sweet Solitude	1.5m	198
Scents on the Breeze	2.5m	200
Trick or Treat	1.5m	203
Great North Western	1.5m	205
Coming out of my Shell	2m	207
Dark and Stormy Night	2m	210
Framed	1.5m	213
Naughty Step	1.5m	215
Her At Number 7	2.5m	217
Bread Sticks and Custard Slices	2m	220
Number Five	2m	223
Memory	1.5m	226
Lucky Fifty	1.5m	228
The Blank Canvas	2m	230
Scent of Pine	1.5m	233
Tick Tock	1.5m	235
Notes from the author		238
About the author		240

Reading times are based on an average reading speed of 183 words per minute.

Switchback

A magical journey back in time.

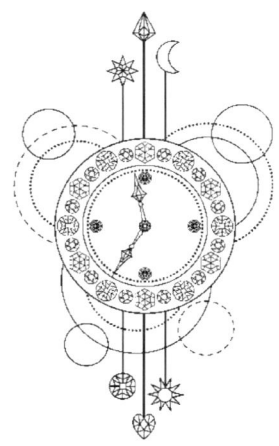

Monday 1st February

Dear Diary, I've nothing much to report, it's been yet another boring day. I wish I hadn't stayed up so late last night; I had to get through a day's work on just five hours of sleep. I survived the battle of getting the girls through their homework. Why do we waste half an hour arguing over homework? They know it has to be done and I end up evil mum for making them do it. I'm sure I was never this belligerent with my parents. Well, the little monsters are finally in bed and I have a week's worth of chores to catch up on. I'm so tired. I know I should get an early night but I also know I'll end up crashing out on the sofa watching some trash on TV. When will I ever learn?

Oh Diary, I wish there was some escape from this drudgery. Anything. I'm just so weary of my life.

Tuesday 2nd February

Dear Diary, what's going on? It's Tuesday, right? I'm so confused. Yesterday was Monday. I went to work as usual. I got up ridiculously early this morning to get ready for the early shift at work. I went about my routine, finally creeping up to kiss the girls goodbye. The little ones grumbled and pulled their covers over their heads, but Sasha woke to ask where I was going. She looked at me like I was stupid and pointed out that it's Saturday. Saturday? Can't be. I turned on my mobile to check the time as I rushed out the door—I was late as usual—it said Saturday! I ran back inside, up the stairs, and woke Chris. He wasn't impressed to be woken at 6:30am on the weekend. Yes, he angrily confirmed it is definitely the weekend. I ran round the house checking alarm clocks, the TV news, and my phone again. I even rung work, but it went through to the answerphone. It is Saturday the 30th of January. How can that be? Did I dream the next few days? If I did dream them, I also appear to have written my diary while sleeping – sleep-writing, that's a new skill!

Hey Diary, me again. I'm still confused, and it's still Saturday. I'm seriously losing the plot, Diary. The only thing I can think is that this is all some weird dream. I was wide awake after my early morning date checking madness, so ran round catching up on all the chores I meant to do last night. By the time Chris and the girls wandered down, I'd blitzed the kitchen, tidied the living room and was on my second load of washing. Last Saturday, (today...?) the first time round we had such a lazy day. We lounged around in pyjamas; the girls got bored and bickered constantly, but by the time we could be bothered to move, it was too late to go out. By some weird magic I don't quite understand, I have an opportunity to do the day over. I'm not going to waste it. But I'm still not convinced this isn't all some bizarre dream.

*****

We had such an amazing day. We packed a picnic, wellies and waterproofs and spent the day out in the fresh air. Layla and Tilly splashed in every puddle, and Sasha made a friend on the playground. It's been such a lovely family day and so nice to come home to a tidy house. I'm exhausted now so I am actually going to get an early night. Fresh sheets too – bliss!

Wednesday 3rd February

Dear Diary, yesterday was weird! It is Wednesday - I know; I checked as soon as I woke up. I mentioned to Chris about what a fantastic day we'd had, but he raised his eyebrow in disbelief and muttered something about work. I asked Sasha if she'd enjoyed yesterday; she gave me THAT look. For an eight-year-old, she really has perfected the teenage eye roll. Apparently, while I was splashing in puddles and admiring the view, she was at school. Bizarre!

The house was back to the same old state and the pile of dirty washing seemed to have doubled again. Ah well, it must have been a dream, a strange one, but a dream, nonetheless. What I can't fathom is why I wrote such a clear description in this diary. It was fun but I'm relieved things are back to normal.

Hey Diary, I got the chores done and I'm off for an early night. This is the new me!

Thursday 4th February

Diary, it's happening again. I woke for work but I'm in a tent! What the hell is going on? A quick peep out of the door has revealed I'm in a woodland. And I'm wearing a onesie! I don't know whether to crawl back into my sleeping bag and wake up back in my real life or pull on some wellies and enjoy the morning sunshine.

*****

Right Diary, I really don't understand what's happening but for some reason, this diary is confirming what I believe is going on. If I am losing my mind, I should perhaps leave myself some reminders of who I am. Here goes...

My name is Cassy, I am forty-three; I am married to Chris, and we have three children—Sasha aged eight, Layla aged six and little Tilly aged four.

Thankfully, I can get a signal out here; a quick check of my mobile reveals it's July 31st last year. I've gone back in time six months. How mad is that? Well Diary, I can waste time puzzling over this or make the most of another bizarre day.

*****

Wow Diary, what an amazing day! I managed to rekindle the embers in the campfire and made a big mug of coffee. I had over an hour of peaceful contemplation, sat on a log at the fireside. I listened to the woodland wake up; the breeze shushing the leaves, the early birds calling and somewhere beyond the edges of the trees, lambs bleated. Soon though, the quiet was filled with excited chatter as the girls bounded out of the tent. We spent the day pottering around, well I pottered as the girls ran, jumped, climbed, and scurried through the undergrowth. We took a walk across the field to the farm. Two new lambs ran down the path to greet us and the girls were delighted. The farmer let them collect eggs from the very free-range hens that cooed around our feet.

It was such a clear night, a full moon; we took the blanket down to the field to watch the stars. An idyllic day. I wonder where or when I will wake up tomorrow. I don't mind going crazy if every day is like today.

Friday 5th February

Dear Diary, I'm disappointed to discover it is the 5th of February. I am forty-three, mum of Sasha, Layla and Tilly, and married to Chris. I'm losing my mind, but I'm having great fun along the way. And I'm talking to a diary!

*****

Well, today was as mundane as expected, but at least it's Friday. I vow to not waste my weekend but for now I'm going to relax. Let's see what tomorrow brings.

Saturday 6th February

Dear Diary, I'm so excited, it is indeed Saturday but not the Saturday I was expecting. I am forty, today, it's my birthday! Not that the 6th of Feb is my actual birthday, but logic seems to have left my life right now. If I remember rightly, we're off to a barbecue party at a local reservoir.

I was right. I also remembered there would be a freak rainstorm, so I bagged the barbecue with the shelter as soon as we got there. Sure enough, we'd just finished eating when the heavens opened. Instead of huddling under the shelter with the other grown-ups, this time I danced in the rain with the children.

Oh Diary, what is happening to me? It seems I can change the day. If only I knew the date in advance, I could check out the lottery numbers or something. There appears to be a pattern, the real day followed by a switch back in time, then back to a real day. Is this going to continue? If I'm right, I should have an ordinary Sunday tomorrow. We'll soon see.

Sunday 7th February

Ha ha Diary, I was right! It is Sunday and I am back to being forty-three.

I don't want to waste any more precious time, so I got up early and had the school uniform washed, ironed and hung out ready for Monday before 10am. With homework done by 10.30am (a miracle in our house) we had a whole day to go out and have fun. We took the girls for a play in the park, then went to my mum's house for dinner.

Diary, I am enjoying these strange time switches, but it does worry me a little. I mean, if I'm in the past, who is being me in the present? I tentatively quizzed Chris about how I'd been behaving, but he just said I seemed happier. He got that right, but I'm still none the wiser. Nobody seems to have noticed anything out of the ordinary. That's a bit scary, but how can I find out for sure without sounding completely crazy? If my theory is correct, tomorrow should be a switch-back day. I'm so excited!

Monday 8th February

Switch-back day.

Dear Diary, I am getting the hang of this now. First stop, check the date. I couldn't believe how long it took my old phone to come on. It makes you appreciate the improvements made to technology. Anyway, I digress. I am Cassy and today I am thirty-nine. I'm snuggling in bed with a newly born baby Tilly. Ah, that newborn smell. It brings tears to my eyes as I breathe in her wispy curls and kiss her forehead tenderly. I'm not wasting time writing in here....

Tuesday 9th February

Just another boring Tuesday.... Can't wait to see where and when I wake up tomorrow. Unless the pattern changes, odd days are real days and even days are switch-backs. I'm going further back in time with each one - scary! I wonder how far I'll go. Will it stop or is this my life from now on? Seriously, Diary, if I wasn't writing this down, I wouldn't believe it.

Wednesday 10th February

Switch-back day.

OMG diary! I'm thirty-five, in hospital and about to give birth! Seriously? I get the opportunity to redo a day and you make me go through childbirth again?

First contraction... can't write... see you on the other side, Diary.

I have a girl! My little Sasha is here! Well, I already knew that, but it feels like I'm experiencing it for the first time - again. (As far as everyone else is concerned, I am!) First time around I didn't know what to do, my mind worried about all the 'what ifs?' and I struggled to push her out. I don't need a diary entry to remind me of that pain! This time, my internal muscles responded with the experience of birthing three children. In fact, the midwife commented that it was the easiest first baby she'd attended! Apparently, I'm a natural - if only they knew! When I look at this tiny helpless baby, and think of the beautiful, quirky child she's going to grow into...how many mums get to know their child before they're grown? This is mind-blowing and I'm so emotional. No more today, Diary, I can't waste a minute more.

Thursday 11th February

Oh wow, Diary, yesterday was AMAZING! Once the girls were back from school, I dragged out the old photo albums. Cuddled on the sofa, we giggled over baby pictures – Sasha perched on a tree branch, too high for her years, toddler Layla stomping in a puddle, mud dripping down her laughing face, and Tilly, my little bundle of cuteness snuggled in her crib. The girls humoured me for a bit, then demanded TV – Peppa Pig reruns, a rare form of parental torture!

Friday 12th February

Switch-back day.

OMG Diary, I'm huge! At a guess, I'd say I was nearly five months pregnant. Checking dates and my old diary, I discovered today was the day I felt the baby move for the first time. I remember now; I didn't realise what it was at first, and Chris missed it. I can change that!

Dear Diary, I'm in tears again. I feel so blessed to revisit this moment. And I made sure Chris was with me to share it. Precious moments….

Saturday 13th February

Hey, Diary! It occurred to me that the only constant thing in these crazy switch-back days is you. Everything else is as it was, except I have my current diary with me – weird! Looking back at the old diaries, the entries are the same. Nothing seems to have changed except I get to do over the day. Would I know if it had changed, though? These thoughts are troubling me. What if I do something in the past that completely changes my future? So far that doesn't seem the case…but what if…?

Sunday 14th February

Switch-back day.

It's Valentine's Day and I'm getting married again! Rather apt, especially seeing as I got married in August the first time around. I wonder what my other self is doing today in the real world. I can't believe how young I look at thirty-three! No more writing, I'm just going to stop worrying about how this is happening and enjoy the day. How many people get to marry the same person twice?

Monday 15th February

There doesn't seem to be any logic to the time jumps in these switch-backs. The only consistency is that I'm going further back in time with each switch. If this continues, will I cease to exist? Will I discover previous lives? Mind-boggling! I'm simultaneously excited and terrified about where this is going. I've gone back ten years in the last fortnight!

It seems to only switch back to significant dates – wedding, first kicks, giving birth etc. I'm wracking my brain for what could be next. So far, they've all been amazing experiences, but there are plenty of times I never want to revisit. Please Diary, let it be something nice tomorrow.

Tuesday 16th February

Switch-back day.

I'm twenty-eight and according to my old diary, there's nothing special happening today. On the original day, I met up with my dad in town, went shopping, then we went for a coffee together. It was pleasant, but not some great life-changing moment....

Of course, Diary, I get it! My dad! He's alive and I get to spend another day with him. It's about a year before he knew he was ill. By the time he knew, it was too late. Can I change it? If I get him to see the doctor now, will they have time to cure him? I have to try.

Dear Diary, thank you for this day. Such a bitter /sweet experience. He was a little perplexed at my emotional greeting, but I didn't care. Such an ordinary day made extraordinary by the knowledge I have. I told him he must go get checked out by a doctor for the headaches he's getting. He laughed it off. What else could I say? 'Dad, I've travelled back from the future in a weird switch-back....' Like he would have believed that! I guess I'll find out tomorrow.

Wednesday 17th February

Dear Diary, it didn't work. I've pulled a sickie from work. How can I explain that I'm grieving for my dad, who died fifteen years ago? Yesterday was amazing and I will always cherish the memory. I know in time I will look back and appreciate it, but today, the hurt of losing him again is just too much to bear. I can't write any more.

Thursday 18th February

Switch-back day.

Oh my god, Diary! I'm so young and skinny! I'm twenty-four and at Glastonbury Festival. The atmosphere is electric. So many people. I'm not used to being this sociable and I can't believe my younger self used to wear such tight jeans – it's been a while since I fit into a size 8! I suspect I won't get to write much more. I'm going to make the most of every second. Wow, this is amazing!!!

Friday 19th February

Slow down please, Diary. I'm exhausted. I mean, it's such an awesome opportunity to experience the highlights of my life, but I'm losing sense of who I am. Where will I be tomorrow? Where was I today when I should have been here with my children? Still, nobody has noticed anything strange and that in itself is mind-bogglingly strange. I just can't get my head around it.

They say people's lives flash before their eyes as they die… am I dying?

Saturday 20th February

Switch-back day.

So, Diary… I'm nineteen, at uni, and I'm away from home for the first time. Life's too short for diaries…. PARTY!!!

Sunday 21st February

Diary, I'm rapidly running out of time. How long can this go on before I cease to exist?

Monday 22nd February

Switch-back day.

Hey, Diary! I'm fifteen and I'm leaving school today! I can't wait to see my old friends again.

OMG Diary! That was awesome! I saw Liz, Tammy and Caroline, my bestest buddies. It was a little sad too. While we were hugging and promising to stay in touch forever, I knew it wouldn't happen. Back in the real world, we all went off to uni, got jobs and moved on. Still, with the atmosphere of leaving school and a full summer ahead, nobody questioned my emotional hugs. Thank you, Diary.

Tuesday 23rd February

Spending a day with my old school friends has made me nostalgic. By the magic of social media, I've found them! It's almost like no time has passed – we just picked up where we left off. This time, I vow not to lose touch. I just hope I have some time left.

Wednesday 24th February

Switch-back day.

Hello Diary, I'm ten and I have to go to school, but it is OK cos today is sports day. I am really, really good at sports.

I won the running race, and I came second in the hurdles. My mum and dad came to watch, and they cheered when I got my medal. My friend Ali came to my house after, and we played out in the garden. Then Mum made us sausages with mash and spaghetti shapes for tea.

Thursday 25th February

Dear Diary, I'm rapidly running out of time. I don't know how many more switch-backs I can do. If I cease to exist in the past, do I cease to exist here? Just in case...

Dear Chris, if you are reading this, I need you to go back to the beginning of February and read the whole month – it will explain everything. You may not believe it, but it's all true. Please know that I love you and the girls very much.

Friday 26th February

Switch-back day.

It is my birfday and I am 6. Mummy and daddy got me a new bike and some Legos. I played with my friends. We had cake. It was a good day.

Saturday 27th February

Aww Diary, that was such a sweet day. Just six more years to switch back. I'm so nervous….

Sunday 28th February

I am free.

Monday 29th February

Hey Diary, I'm still here. I remember asking my dad to spell out, 'I am three' yesterday, but looking back, he must have misheard me. It took so long to copy out those letters, three-year-old me got bored and went off playing. It was such a peculiar experience. I knew deep down that I wasn't supposed to be there, but my toddler brain overrode the doom of my impending non-existence. I ran, I climbed, I felt the wind whip through my tangled curls, and I laughed. Oh Diary, it's been a while since I laughed like that.

This may be my last entry. I feel strangely at peace with the situation. There's no point in worrying about whether there will be a tomorrow. I'm going to make the most of the time I have left.

Chris, Sasha, Layla, Tilly, I love you so much.

Tuesday 1st March

I'm still here, Diary! Today should have been a switch-back day, but it's a normal Tuesday. Has it stopped? Or has it skipped the first of March because it's an odd number? Was this some weird leap year thing? I don't want to be too hopeful…tomorrow will tell.

Wednesday 2nd March

Dear Diary, I am here, and it is Wednesday the 2nd of March. Never have I been so relieved to wake up on a workday.

It seems it is over. I don't know whether to be happy or sad – relieved certainly! I have no control over the passing of time and life can be strange, but each moment is precious. You never realise as it's happening that it may be the last moment you spend with someone, or the last time you will experience something. I feel blessed to have had this experience, though it has been simultaneously exhilarating and perplexing. I read back through February. Already it seems unreal but the memories, together with these diary entries, confirm I didn't dream it. Or maybe I did, but how do I explain the switch-back days in my diary? Maybe I'm dreaming now…. Will I ever discover what went on in the present on the days I was revisiting the past? Life sure is strange, Diary! Maybe I'll never get answers to all my questions.

I keep going back to the last switch-back day – I am free – maybe it wasn't a spelling error after all. No more worries, no more wasting time. I am free!

Murky Windows

New house, new challenges, new ways.

Moira paused with the key in the lock and checked the time on her phone - 15:57. She glanced around to make sure none of the neighbours were watching. This was a memorable moment, and she wanted to wait for a 'nice' time. She giggled at her own silliness, but still waited. 15:59 - mentally counting down the seconds, she turned the doorknob.... 16:00 - and open.

The grime of neglect was the only thing to dull Moira's spirits as she threw open the door of their new home. The action caused a flurry of activity, as spiders scurried back into cobwebby corners and dust motes sparkled in the beam of sunlight through the stone doorway. She smiled at the quirky little cottage with its wonky wooden beams and uneven plaster walls. A good cleaning, and maybe a fresh lick of paint, was all it needed to return to its former glory.

Moira skirted around the packing boxes and bits of furniture the movers had left. Smiling again, she noted her meticulous labelling had not been in vain. The furniture, though shoved randomly to the side of each room, was at least in the rooms she had planned. It would save her a lot of trouble, meaning she could clean and unpack everything before the family moved in.

Mac often laughed at her obsessive behaviour - what she called 'meticulous', he lovingly called her OCDness. At the beginning of the relationship, it was a battle, his mess versus her need for order. His persistent lateness versus her need to be on time. They'd both compromised as the years went by, but there were certain things Moira wouldn't budge on, and this was one of them. She knew it would've driven her mad to clean and unpack if the family were there tramping dust through and randomly opening boxes.

Most people would be daunted by the prospect of unpacking a family home unaided, but Moira was secretly thrilled to have a week to do everything her way. Besides, they had one week of the lease left on the old place, and the kids still had a week of school before the summer holidays started. Mac and the kids were equally excited to spend a week on camp beds in the living room of the now empty old house, and no doubt they would be living off take-aways for every meal. Mac had kept behind just a few basics to keep them going until he locked up the old house for good.

Moira got out her list, another one of her OCDnesses that Mac loved to poke fun at. She had worked out a plan of action, the optimum order of unpacking, and the first on the list was the kettle. She walked through the living room to the kitchen at the back. It overlooked the garden through a big window and a glass-paned door. She quickly located the right box, and retrieved the kettle, her favourite mug, coffee, and teaspoons. She'd bought fresh milk and food at the supermarket on the way. She made the coffee and ticked off the first item on the list.

Peering through the grimy window to the garden beyond, she mused that getting a window cleaner might have to be bumped further up her list of tasks. The rooms would look so much brighter with sparkling clean windows. It was too big a task for her to master. She made a mental note to ask a neighbour who the local window cleaner was. In a small village like this, it made sense to use a local business and would help them fit in.

Moira carried her coffee upstairs. Her next task was to get the master bedroom sorted. All she really needed was her bed made, and her toiletries unpacked, then she could settle in for an early night with her book. It would mean she could be up fresh and early the next day to make a proper start on the rest of the cottage. Moira worked tirelessly, stopping only for a quick bite to eat, until she had the bedroom more or less straight. It had been harder work than she thought to wrestle a king-size mattress into place. Finally, she tossed her dusty clothes in the wash basket and flopped down onto the bed, exhausted. She checked the time 21:21 precisely—perfect! The rest could be sorted tomorrow.

The alarm went off at 07:00, Moira hit the snooze button and buried her face in the pillow. Beep, beep, beep. 07:07, she sat up and turned off the alarm. She missed the familiar ribbing from Mac - "seven minutes past? Why can't you just snooze your alarm in five-minute intervals, like normal people?" Moira grinned. She liked even numbers, repetitive patterns and especially palindromic numbers. Mac thought she was nuts - she didn't care!

It should have been lighter at this time of day. Moira wandered over to the window, admiring the new curtains she'd hung the day before, as she swooshed them open. This room looked out over the garden too, or it would do if the windows weren't so grubby. She made another mental note to book a window cleaner. It was such a shame to have this view obscured by mildew and dust. In fact, the upstairs windows seemed worse than the downstairs ones.

The excitement of creating a home from the piles of boxes spurred Moira on. During a quick breakfast and a coffee - she reviewed the list and ticked off last night's completed tasks. Today, she would tackle the kitchen, but first, a trip to the local shop for fresh milk and a few other essentials.

The local shop was a bakery/ newsagent /supermarket /post office combined. With a cash machine outside too, there was everything she needed within walking distance. Moira noted the time taken to walk there—two minutes and 32 seconds precisely. It certainly beat the half hour round trek in traffic to the supermarket at their last home in Stockport. Alder Green was such a pretty little place. The shop and the pub opposite were the same black and white style as the cottages that surrounded the village green. Further down the road, the school was a more modern building, but it had been painted to blend in. She could hear the chatter of the children in the playground—08:45—they would soon be going into lessons.

Moira became aware of the glances from other shoppers, as she browsed round the veggie aisle. She smiled back and caught the eye of the lady nearest to her.

"You're new here. Arthur's place?" said the woman, when she realised she'd been caught staring.

Moira must have looked confused….

"Number 3. Arthur Ryder used to live there."

"Oh, I didn't know that," Moira replied. "Yes, we've just moved into number 3. Well, I have. I'm getting everything sorted for when the family moves in next week. I'm Moira."

The lady introduced herself as Gladys from number 9 and proceeded to fill Moira in on the local gossip. Other locals drifted round once Gladys had started, and soon, Moira felt she knew the life histories of most of the village. Gladys seemed particularly proud to be the first to talk to her.

"I wonder if you can give me the name of the local window cleaner," Moira addressed the gaggle of women.

"Billy Dobbs," they said in unison.

"Yeah, everyone in Alder Green uses Billy. We have a lovely, safe village and we want to keep it that way," Gladys explained. The other ladies nodded and murmured their agreement.

It seemed a strange answer, but Moira mused she hadn't got used to village ways yet. After answering questions about her children and where they used to live, Moira finally managed to politely prise herself away. Gladys promised to send Billy along and warned that she'd likely get a visit from Hatty—whoever she was.

Moira smiled as she scurried home with her purchases. It had taken rather longer than she'd planned, but it was good to suss out some of the village characters. She made a quick coffee, then got on with the list. Next job - the kitchen.

Moira worked methodically, ticking off chores as she completed them. It pleased her to see the cottage slowly being transformed. As she hung curtains in the front room, a face popped up, beaming from the other side of the grimy glass.

"Billy, Billy Dobbs. Window cleaner…" the man shouted and waved a bucket.

Moira quickly opened the door and introduced herself to the rather aged man—he looked to be close to retiring from the window cleaning business. He was small and wiry with leathery skin, no doubt from working outside, and his wide grin revealed a few gaps between his nicotine-stained teeth. Billy gave her his business card—a handwritten scrawl photocopied onto regular paper and cut down to business card size—and agreed to get to work straight away.

Moira left Billy to it and got back on with the curtains. She'd just finished hanging the second set when there was a knock on the door. Billy stood there smiling, bucket in hand and one wet trouser leg. Moira really hoped it was water and tried not to look.

"That was quick! How much do I owe you?"

Billy beamed. "Fastest cleaner in the village!" he said proudly. "A fiver'll do it. Thanks, love."

Moira handed over a five-pound note, thanked him, and carried on. As she was hanging the third curtain, she realised she hadn't seen or heard him clean any of the windows of the room she was in. A quick look round the downstairs rooms, and she saw the results of Billy's efforts—the grime had been pushed around with a damp cloth, leaving a few clean smears between the grubby bits. She ran upstairs to check, expecting the same shoddy work, but found the windows no different than before. Thinking about it, she didn't recall seeing a ladder when she was handing over her money.

If anything, the windows looked worse than before. Grabbing the scrawled business card, she started to tap the mobile number into her phone, then stopped. Her initial anger at having paid for such a shoddy job, half a shoddy job even, was replaced with the acceptance that this was village life. What was expected and acceptable in Stockport was very different here. It was probably better to just organise a proper cleaner, she mused. There was no need to berate Billy and risk antagonising the village folk. A quick search found a company in the next village and soon she had a booking for the following day.

The next morning, brought a stream of visitors. First off was Gladys, armed with a tray of scones. Moira invited her in, apologising about the mess. Clearing a few boxes off the sofa, she made room for her nosy neighbour to sit down while she made coffee.

"I see Billy's been," Gladys shouted through to the kitchen.

"Er, yes…. He's not, er…very professional, is he?" said Moira, trying to think of the best way to describe the redistribution of grime.

Gladys chuckled as Moira handed her a coffee. "No, our Billy isn't what he used to be. But we all use him for the good of the village."

"But aren't you bothered about paying for this?" she replied, gesturing towards a mucky corner of the window.

"Now, you've got to understand that village ways are different from the big city where you come from."

Moira would hardly call Stockport a big city, but by comparison, it was huge. She shrugged. She decided not to mention Squeaky Kleen, who was due to call later in the day.

Next to call was Mr Potts, bearing a punnet of freshly picked raspberries from his allotment, and an invitation to visit anytime. He politely refused the offer to come in, explaining that his runner beans needed trimming. Moira was secretly relieved he wouldn't be tramping muddy wellies across her newly swept floor.

Moira was beginning to think she'd never get through the day's chores when she heard a third knock at the door. Expecting the window cleaners, she rushed down, but was confronted by an elderly woman, all dressed up as if she was off to some posh function. Moira could see behind the lavishly applied makeup that she'd been an attractive woman in her youth. Now, she just looked gaudy against the quaint old cottages.

"Pleased to make your acquaintance. Harriet Dawbs, church secretary and neighbourhood watch," she said in an overly posh accent that almost hid the country twang.

Moira smiled back kindly, held open the door and swept her arm back, welcoming in her guest. It seemed village life included having a nosy round the houses of all newcomers.

With polite introductions made, Harriet plumped the cushion and settled herself down on the sofa.

"I'd like to welcome you to Alder Green. My husband and I have lived here since we were married, and I know everything there is to know about the village and its residents." Harriet sat back, nibbled a scone, then brushed the crumbs from her tweed skirt.

Moira managed to suppress a giggle. She bet that Harriet was the local busybody. She started to reply, but Harriet continued.

"My William is the manager of a thriving business that serves the whole of Alder Green…"

"Oh…" started Moira, only to be cut off again.

"And my boys, they're such good boys you know, they both have jobs in Stockport!"

Moira nodded. It seemed Harriet wasn't interested in a two-way conversation.

"They're in the Handiwork and Removals business, you know. Such good boys to their mama. Every day without fail, they go off working hard, then home on the last train in time for tea. They never miss a home-cooked meal."

Moira listened to the stream of accomplishments of Darren and Barry and was relieved when Harriet drained the last sip of coffee.

"Well, I haven't time to sit chatting all day. Will we be seeing you in church on Sunday?"

"Er, I'm not sure… I mean, I have a lot to do at the moment…." Moira faltered, not wanting to explain that the only time she entered a church was for weddings or funerals.

"Of course, I understand. I shall call back at six-thirty tomorrow after choir practice then, and give you details of all the services you can attend."

Completely bamboozled, Moira thanked Harriet and saw her to the door. As she watched the old busy body bustle back towards the shop, a van pulled up outside and stopped—Squeaky Kleen emblazoned along the side. At least one job would get done today, Moira mused as she watched the young man unload a ladder, squeegees and sponges from the back of the van. Already she could tell it was clearly a more professional outfit than Billy and his mucky bucket.

Moira's phone beeped - it was a short video clip from Mac that showed the children snuggled down in sleeping bags, watching something on the laptop. Amber and Oli seemed thrilled with the experience, but it gave her a pang of loneliness. Although she'd had a stream of visitors, it wasn't the same as spending time with her family, and she missed the kids. It was also a beautiful day, so Moira decided to ditch the chores for the rest of the day and go for a wander instead. She wanted to suss out the train times, hoping that she could meet the children after school and take them out for tea.

Old habits ingrained; Moira checked the time. Six minutes later, she arrived at the train station on the other side of the school. Well, it wasn't much more than a platform with a shed. A quick check of the timetable revealed that although she had plenty of time to do the 28-minute journey there, the last train back from Stockport would leave at 17:00—not enough time for her to take the kids out for tea if she picked them up at 15:30. She decided to take the car instead. That way, she wouldn't be rushing.

There was plenty of time before she'd need to leave, so Moira ambled back around the other side of the Green. The route took her past a garage and then the allotments. She waved at Mr Potts over the canes of sweet peas. He waved back and shouted her over. Pleasantries aside, and a request to call him Albert, he proudly gave a tour of his patch. Albert picked a plump pod of peas and handed it to Moira.

"I hear you met our Batty Hatty," Albert said with a chuckle.

"Hatty? Oh, do you mean Harriet Dawbs?"

"Yep, Hatty Dobbs, wife of Billy and local nosy parker!" Albert carried on wandering down the rows of crops as he chatted, occasionally picking a ripe raspberry or strawberry for Moira to sample.

"Ah, I see. Yes, I had the official visit from Hatty and the lecture about her two angelic sons."

"Bah! Angelic? Baz and Daz are, and have always been, thieving little gits." Albert shook his head. "They caused no end of trouble in the village…trashed my shed, trampled all over my lettuces…. Not to mention the break-ins!"

"Really?" Moira replied in surprise. The village seemed like such a quiet place to live.

"Yep, the gits used to be part of the family window cleaning business, but 'coincidentally', stuff went missing every time they cleaned. Not too bright, those two. Didn't take long for PC Davies to make the connection."

"But everyone still uses Billy…and he's…." Moira faltered.

"He's flipping useless!" Albert finished for her. "It seems that the only ones blinkered to Baz and Daz's antisocial activities are Billy and Hatty. And we're happy to keep it that way for the good of the village."

"I don't understand. I mean, why would you continue using Billy, and how did PC Davies stop them? Why does everyone keep saying, 'for the good of the village'?" Moira was trying to keep up with village ways, but it seemed a strange setup.

"Well, Baz and Daz have little respect for anyone, but they're terrified of upsetting their dear mama," Albert chucked. "I suspect it's more they don't want to lose their cushy lifestyle - Old Hatty dotes on that pair and thinks the sun shines out of their…well, you get the picture."

"I think I'm beginning to, but it still doesn't explain why they're suddenly working in Stockport, and Billy is continuing to smear grime around the village windows," Moira replied.

"Well, PC Davies had a little chat…. The stolen goods miraculously appeared in the church office for Hatty to find - she revelled in the glory of having solved the problem by praying for the thief to repent."

Moira giggled; she could just imagine the self-righteous old bat crowing to all who'd listen.

"Baz and Daz were told to clear off and get jobs elsewhere, in return for keeping their mum none the wiser. Everyone in the village knows apart from the Dobbs."

"OK...but isn't that just moving the problem elsewhere?"

Albert shrugged. "It works for the village, and we've been relatively crime free ever since."

"But what about Billy?" Moira asked, still slightly confused about the vagaries of village life.

"Well, at first Billy was against the idea of the boys leaving the family business. We all convinced him that he could manage on his own without the boys. He carried on for a bit, but after he fell from the ladder, Hatty banned him from using it again - and Billy always does as Hatty says. He was going to bring the boys back into the business again, so we had a village meeting. We all agreed that paying Billy to do half a job was better than the alternative. Unfortunately, he got worse with age—it comes to us all."

"Ah, I see," Moira said, pondering the strange situation. It seemed she still had a lot to learn about village ways. It was an odd way to deal with thieves, but if it kept harmony in the village, it suited her fine.

Moira said her goodbyes and made her way home. She was greeted by the Squeaky Kleen guys who were just packing the last bits into the van. Feeling slightly guilty, Moira admired her shiny, clean windows. The whole house looked brighter and better for a thorough clean. It spurred her on to get a few jobs done before she drove back to Stockport to pick up the children.

At exactly 15:25, Moira stood outside the school gates, waiting for the bell to go. The five minutes felt like an eternity, but it was worth the wait to see the grins on Amber's and Oli's faces. Moira drove them to the local pub, where they would meet Mac. It was a great family pub with a big garden outside, which meant the kids could play while the food was on order - that's if they stopped talking long enough to breathe. The way they were babbling, it felt like they'd been apart for several weeks.

Eventually, exhausted of filling in their mum about their adventures camping in the old house, the children ran off to the climbing frames. Moira was just studying the menu when Mac arrived. She hugged Mac and proceeded to tell him everything about the strange quirks of village life. Seeing his bemused grin, Moira realised she was babbling just as much as the kids had.

The family ate well. Then Amber and Oli begged to go back and play with the new friends they'd made. Moira sighed and sipped her drink as she watched the daredevil pair leaping from the climbing frame - it wouldn't be long before they were all back together in the new cottage.

Moira's phone beeped. 17:57, she noted as she checked the message, then cried out in dismay.

"What's the matter?" Mac asked. He took the phone from Moira and studied the photo, which filled the screen.

Moira's anti-theft software on her laptop (the laptop that should have been sitting on her desk) had sent a blurry photo of the person who was currently inputting the wrong code. Although it was hard to tell who it was, it was definitely not Moira, and that was not her floral wallpaper in the background.

"Damn! Looks like I'm going to have to head straight back. I'll ring PC Davies en route."

"Do you want me to come with you?" Mac queried, concerned. "I can follow you in my car...."

"No, you get the kids home. There's no need to worry them. If I can't sort it, I'll secure the house and drive back here."

With regret, Moira hugged her family and set off on the journey home. PC Davies agreed to meet her at the house.

Moira's heart sunk as she surveyed the damage. The back door had been kicked in, and the kitchen trashed. PC Davies appeared as she was gingerly stepping over her smashed coffee jar. Together, they followed footprints in the coffee granules. The living room was just as bad as the kitchen, but a quick scout round showed that no other rooms had been touched, and the only thing that seemed to be missing was her laptop.

Moira righted the sofa and slumped down, inviting PC Davies to join her.

"So, what's the village procedure for dealing with this?" Moira said with a defeated sigh.

"Well, it's strange. We haven't had a break-in like this in years. I'm supposed to be retiring next week—just typical we get trouble now of all times. We've got some hotshot from Stockport taking over—PC Mo Smith, I think his name is—I'll take down your details now, but I guess it'll be him dealing with it."

Moira grinned, despite the situation, it was an amusing turn of events that brought PC Davies to her house.

While PC Davies got out his notepad, Moira found the photo on her phone and held it out to him. "Whoever it was, tried unsuccessfully to unlock my laptop."

"Well, I'll be damned!" Davies shook his head. "That looks like Baz Dobbs, and if he was here, his brother wouldn't have been too far away. I'll be having a little chat with the Dobbs brothers. Right, let's get your details, then we'll sort it. I wonder what set those two off thieving again...."

The sun shone through the sparkling clean windows and caused PC Davies to squint as he wrote the date and time on the top of the page. He glanced at the window and a moment of revelation flashed across his eyes.

"Our Billy didn't do that, did he?"

Moira shifted uncomfortably. "Er no, he did attempt to do them but, well, I wasn't happy, so I got another company to do them properly."

"I think we've uncovered the reason you got the Dobbs' treatment. Those two are very protective of their dad. OK, let's get these details down and I'll go have a chat."

"Moira, Moira Smith, but Mo to my colleagues," she grinned. "The hotshot from Stockport! Look, I know officially you're still in charge, but would you mind if I dealt with this one? It seems I still have some learning to do about village ways."

PC Davies chuckled. "Of course, it'd be my pleasure. How do you want to play this?"

"On your way back, call at the Dobbs' residence and suggest the boys pop round to see me. I have an idea that might be mutually beneficial."

Baz and Daz Dobbs reluctantly knocked on the front door just seven minutes later. Moira invited them in, making a show of stepping over the upended boxes. "So, it seems somebody has trashed my house and nicked my laptop."

"Nowt do with us, lady," one of the pair snapped.

"Well, here's what I think: you got back from work, nipped home to hear your mum gossiping about how the newcomer had got someone else in to clean the windows. So, you popped right over to rearrange the furniture and help yourselves to a new laptop. Am I close?"

"Wasn't us and you can't prove nothin'," the other of the pair said.

"Well, that's where you're wrong." Moira turned her phone around, displaying the blurry photo.

"Bah, you can't tell who it is from that pic. Besides, couldn't have been us, we was working in Stockport."

"Yeah, not long been back. No proof, not our problem," the second Dobbs brother chipped in. They both turned to leave.

"Okay...you see, I'm a bit of a stickler for time. The last train arrived in at 17:28—let's call it 17:30. It takes three and a half minutes to walk from the station to the shop, and I gather you live a couple of doors down from it. Assume five minutes of listening to your mum moan about other window cleaners taking over, then two and a half minutes' walk to my house. You following this, boys? That takes us to 17:41. Let's say six minutes to boot the door in, another six to trash two rooms, two and a half minutes to walk home, and a minute and a half to sneak the laptop past your mother and into your bedroom. That takes us to 17:57—the timestamp on the photograph of your ugly mug."

"Yer still just guessing. Can't prove nothing," Ugly Mug said, shrugging. His brother didn't look too sure, though.

"Hmmm, I guess you're right. Sorry to have troubled you boys. I guess I'll just have to walk back with you and ask our village neighbourhood watch if she recognises who has this rather distinctive floral wallpaper - what do you reckon?"

"OK, OK.... There's no need to bring our mum into this," the boy from the photo shot back, a look of panic spreading across his face.

Moira grinned back at the two white faces. "Here's what's going to happen: first off, you boys help the neighbourhood watch scheme and 'find' my missing laptop. Once it's returned, I'll give PC Davies a call and ask him to forget about filing the report. Then tomorrow morning, you'll appear here with a new jar of coffee, a coffee pot and some tools to fix a busted door. Consider it community service."

One of the brothers nodded, but the other didn't seem to grasp the situation.

"Why should we? We've got work tomorrow."

"Well, it just so happens that your lovely mother is calling round here at six-thirty, after choir practise. It would be an awful shame to have to explain to her how my house came to be in such disarray, now wouldn't it? I think two strong lads like you could easily get that door fixed before my visitor arrives."

The lads sped off and were back in under five minutes with the laptop. Moira grinned as she phoned PC Davies - she was getting used to village ways. She then rang to say goodnight to the children and once they'd gone back to watching TV, she filled Mac in on the Dobbs situation. Mac was uneasy leaving her there alone, but Moira assured him all was fine.

The following day, Baz and Daz appeared bright and early, bringing a battered toolbox and a jar of coffee. They seemed resigned to their fate, and even managed a cheeky grin. Moira left them to it while she cleaned up the mess they'd made—she didn't trust them to do it to her standards.

At 12:30—the start of Mac's lunch break—Moira's phone beeped, signalling a text, but before she could check it, the phone rang. Mac!

"Hi Mo, how's it going with those two scallywags?"

"OK. Actually, they're doing a great job on the door. And so far, they're being respectful," Moira replied.

"That's good. Look, I was thinking last night that the image in your text looked vaguely familiar. I've sent you some pics—have a look and see what you think."

Moira put the call on hold while she looked at the text from Mac—several grainy CCTV stills showed two lads, with caps pulled down to hide their faces. At first glance it was difficult to ID them, but a quick look out of the window confirmed that the Dobbs brothers 'coincidentally' had the same caps and jackets. Not conclusive evidence, but she'd bet that the handiwork and removals business the boys did in Stockport, included breaking in and removing goods from shops like the one the CCTV image was taken from. Moira resumed the call.

"I think your hunch is correct, but there's not enough there to stand up in court. Leave it with me. I have an idea that might solve a few problems and make both our jobs easier."

Moira booted up her laptop and set to work. It was worth putting in a bit of an effort to make her plan work. Finally, she connected the printer, sent her work to print, and put the kettle on. She made a quick call to PC Davies, and he promised to call round in five minutes. Just enough time to brew a pot of tea and put out a plate of biscuits.

At 17:30, Moira called the Dobbs boys in for a break. They looked a little shocked to see PC Davies already sat on the sofa nibbling a digestive biscuit, but they accepted a cup of tea and sat down.

"Firstly, boys, I'd like to thank you for a job well done. You have some decent skills when it comes to handiwork," Moira started.

Both Dobbs brothers grinned and relaxed back with their tea.

"But that brings me onto your other 'handiwork' business…. You see, we have two problems we need to solve if we're all to live happily in this village. But first perhaps I should formally introduce myself—PC Moira Smith, soon to be taking over from PC Davies here."

"Oh man! If we'd known you was a copper…." Baz started, then groaned.

PC Davies chuckled; he was clearly loving seeing the boys squirm.

"So, the first problem is your dad's business - it's not really working, is it? The villagers are being kind because they like your dad, but to be fair, he's getting a bit past the window cleaning job, isn't he?"

Baz shrugged, but Daz nodded in resigned agreement.

"But he loves going round the village chatting to folk, and it keeps him from driving our mum mad," Daz said sadly.

"I figured as much, so I've taken the liberty of updating his business to give him a role more suited to his abilities." Moira grabbed the stack of glossy sheets from the printer and handed a copy to each brother, and one to PC Davies. The stylish flyer read:

Dobbs and Sons

Window Cleaning and Handiwork

"But what about…" PC Davies started, nodding over to the brothers.

Moira cut him off with a wave and a wink. "I've got that covered."

"And sons?" Daz queried. "We can't, we've got jobs in Stockport…."

"I'll come to that issue in a minute," Moira replied. PC Davies leant forward, a confused but interested look on his face.

"So, here's how I see the business developing…. Your dad takes on a managerial role, meeting the customers, taking bookings for jobs, collecting the money, etc. That keeps him happy, and more importantly, away from my windows with his grubby rag! Meanwhile, you two talented lads do a proper job of cleaning windows, plus any other odd jobs people may need doing. The people of Alder Green get the job they've paid for, and your dad oversees your work to ensure no 'additional jobs' are undertaken," Moira continued.

"I'm not sure about that, not after the trouble last time," PC Davies interjected.

"Oh, come now, PC Davies, these lads are now reformed characters, ready to do an honest day's work—aren't you lads?"

"Course! Dead trustworthy, we are. But I'm gonna have to say no, 'cos we already got jobs in Stockport," said Daz.

"I'm glad you mentioned Stockport," Moira said with a grin. "I'm sorry to inform you that your current occupation is no longer an option. As of today, you are both unemployed."

"Eh? What ya saying? We got jobs," said Daz, and Baz nodded in agreement.

Moira turned on her phone and flicked to the CCTV pictures. She showed it to PC Davies, but deliberately held it out of sight of the lads. Davies tutted and shook his head.

"It seems you two have been naughty boys in Stockport. And my husband, Sergeant Mac Smith is wondering if I can help ID these two shoplifters caught on camera, numerous times. So, we get to our second problem…. My husband wants to wrap up this case before he moves house at the weekend, and if these thieves were to retire and take on respectable work instead…."

"So, what you're saying is that we do the cleaning job for our dad, or you'll dob us in to hubby?" said Daz.

"Yeah, she's blackmailing us. We could have you done for that, and we got a witness," Baz blurted out.

"Will you shut up and listen for once, Baz!" Daz said, cuffing his brother around the side of his head. "We could do serious time for them supermarket jobs."

"Thank you for confirming my suspicions that you were the two caught on camera," said Moira. "Sergeant Smith is waiting for me to ring back with an answer. We have two options: you continue in your current line of work, the villagers switch to a better window cleaning business, and I have to do my duty as the local copper and 'dob' you in, or we all agree that the past is best left in the past and you move on to new, respectable careers. I will personally recommend your handiwork skills. PC Davies, you'll have a chat with the villagers about the new arrangements—won't you?"

"Of course, it'd be my pleasure to do this last task before I retire. You can count on me to make it right with the village.

I should say though, that if anything should go missing, or as much as a bean is trampled on in the allotment, this agreement is void." PC Davies gave the boys a stern look, then settled back with another biscuit.

"I agree. So, what's it to be?" asked Moira.

"Can we think about it?" Baz asked.

"What's there to think about, you numbskull?" Daz snapped. "She's got us whichever way you look at it."

Moira checked her watch – 17:58. "Sure, you can think about it. It's nearly six O'clock and your mum will be here in half an hour. What shall we tell her? Her darling boys, saviours of the family business? Or her thieving sons, a disgrace to the family name, soon to be doing time? The clock is ticking...."

Earworm

A tale of a troublesome worm.

The ringing phone on the receptionist's desk did nothing to drown out the noise in my head. I'd struggled along for a couple of weeks, but sheer frustration had driven me to make the appointment to see my doctor. If I had to spend another day with cheesy music on a constant loop, I'd be tempted to do a Van Gogh. Seriously, I'd never known tinnitus like it. I'd occasionally had a light whooshing noise, like a miniature waterfall rushing between my ears, but this was more like being stuck in a lift playing an eighties mixtape through tinny speakers.

Instead of the usual waiting room, I'd been politely ushered through to the first-class lounge on the second floor. The plush carpet and comfy sofas were a far cry from the worn carpet tiles and rows of plastic chairs I was used to. Worried about the cost, I queried the receptionist, but she assured me this was all part of the service, and apparently, my doctor had insisted his colleague see me instead.

"Are you sure you have the right person? I usually see Dr Collier. I don't go private. I can't afford private!"

"It's fine. Seriously, don't worry," the receptionist reassured me. "Dr Collier specifically asked that Dr Squire see you. It's more his speciality."

With that, she winked and left the room. I settled into the sofa and sank back against the cushions. The sunlight hit the room at just the perfect angle to spread its cosy warming beams without blinding me. I was just starting to relax when my tinnitus ramped up to a chorus worthy of a standing ovation. I had been pondering whether to stay or go, now I was singing it inside my head – *arrrrghhhh! The sooner I see this doctor, the better.*

I didn't have to wait long, and I was thankful that I hadn't been singing along with the Clash tribute in my head when the doctor appeared. Dr Squire was a small man, only middle-aged, yet he already had tufts of ginger hair growing from his ears. He scampered into the room, beamed, and beckoned me to follow him. I plodded after him, repeating my mantra above the song clashing through my brain – *Dr Squire. Must not call him Dr Squirrel. Squire, not Squirrel....*

The doctor's room was as posh as the waiting room. I glanced around, thinking it was more like the lounge at the Hilton than the village surgery. Oak panelling hid cupboards that no doubt held medical supplies, and above, soft pastel walls were subtly decorated with restful watercolours. In the centre was a bed, with silken privacy drapes hung from the ceiling around three sides, giving it more the feeling of a fourposter—this whole room was designed to make the patient feel relaxed and at ease, except it screamed of money. A wave of panic rushed through me. I was already dreading the cost of the prescription. I certainly couldn't afford to be presented with a bill for private care as well.

"The receptionist did tell you I'm an NHS patient, didn't she? Are you sure I won't be billed for this?" As if I wasn't feeling under pressure enough, the tinnitus morphed into a familiar beat. 'Under Pressure', o*h great, Tinnitus with a sense of humour!*

"Bill? No, no, you won't be billed for this. If it's faulty, you'll get a replacement. All part of the service. Now hop up onto the bed and I'll take a look."

As Bowie and Freddie battled vocally through my brain, I did as he instructed and then tried to relax. The squirrelly doctor positioned a strange contraption with a light and what looked like a magnifying glass close to my head. I tried to take in what he had said, but it didn't quite make sense. It was difficult to focus on anything important with this music, especially as 'Don't Stop Believing' had now started playing through my head. *Is this my subconscious telling me to relax and trust Dr Squire?*

"So, Dr Collier tells me it's in your left ear, that right?"

I nodded, then closed my eyes as Dr Squire peered through the illuminated magnifying glass.

"Interesting...hmmmm. This is not one of ours. Where did you get it fitted?" the doctor flicked the switch on the contraption and looked down at me, perplexed.

"Fitted? I don't understand what you mean. Didn't Dr Collier mention why I'm here? I'm suffering from tinnitus. It's driving me mad." I sat up. 'Don't Stop Believing' faded into 'Time After Time' and I suppressed the urge to sing along.

"I'm afraid I don't quite understand either," Dr Squire replied. "Are you telling me you have no idea why you're hearing music?"

"Well, I assumed it was tinnitus…what is it? Is it bad?" *Maybe there's nothing wrong with my ears. Perhaps I've just lost the plot. I have had a dodgy eighties disco playing through my head for the last couple of weeks. I've gone crazy….*

"Well, let me explain," he said and took a deep breath. "You have what is known as an 'auris vermis' fitted, or more commonly, an earworm. What song is she programmed with? Can you distinguish the tune?"

"What? Earworm? Seriously? Tune?" *Yep! Definitely gone crazy, I'm hearing aging rock stars, and I'm now babbling like an idiot!*

"You truly have no idea what I'm talking about, do you?" Dr Squire said in confusion. "OK, let me show you. Hop down off the bed and look at this."

The doctor pressed one of the wooden panels, a gentle click sounded, and a cupboard door swung open to reveal shelves of glass vials. The singing in my head paused for a moment, then set off with a triumphant, 'Come on Eileen'. I leaned in closer to look, and heard a very faint, but similar sound to the one dancing through my brain, except this one sounded more like classical music, lots of tunes blending together into a high-pitch whine.

"What are those?" I asked, squinting to make out the contents of the vials.

"Those are ear worms. Those little beauties have revolutionised the treatment of tinnitus. Their therapeutic calming effect was first discovered by Dr C. Lynn two years ago. With controlled breeding in a lab, he developed an earworm that, when inserted into the ear, could drown out the annoying sounds produced by the tinnitus with their own song."

"Wait, hang on…you said breeding? These aren't actual worms, are they?" I shook my head in disgust at the thought, then smiled at the ridiculous vision I'd created. *I must have misheard. Surely no credible doctor would insert an actual worm into someone's ear…and where the hell did I get mine from?* The singer in my ear nudged its way back into conscious thought – 'Don't You, Forget About Me….' *How can I forget about you when you're singing in my ear all day? And now I'm having a conversation with an earworm – yep, definitely going crazy.*

Incredulity battled with logic as I listened in astonishment to the squirrelly doctor's excited confirmation of what I feared. I wracked my brain to think about where I could have acquired one from – where do earworms hang out? I tuned back into what the doctor was saying.

"Yes, well, technically, they are more closely related to a beetle than a worm, but they are certainly worm-like in appearance. And they are quite harmless. In fact, they help to improve the health of the ear, feeding on earwax and preventing a build-up, which can exacerbate tinnitus noise."

"Ewww! Can you remove it?" I didn't want to hear any more, either from the doctor or from the noisy, earwax-eating bug in my ear.

"Of course. I can do that now. It's a quick and simple procedure. Hop back up onto the bed for me."

Revulsion and relief vied for attention as my own earworm sang a panicked, 'Going Underground'.

The doctor repositioned his magnifying light over my ear, chattering away while he unwrapped a pair of sterile tweezers. "Most of our stock are trained in classical – it seems the most popular with our customers – but we cover numerous music genres. It's quite a simple, yet amazing system – the baby earworms memorise the first tune played to them as they hatch. The A-Series could only retain thirty seconds, and largely became as annoying as the tinnitus, so they were discontinued. The B-Series had an increased retention of sixty seconds. We're now on the C-Series. They're quite amazing. They can accurately 'sing' around three minutes' worth of any tune." He paused; tweezers poised. "You didn't answer before. Which tune is your earworm trained with?"

"Err, all of them, I think." I wasn't quite sure now that I did have one of Dr C. Lynn's 'amazing' earworms. What I had been dealing with seemed very different from what Dr Squire had described.

"All of them? I'm not sure I follow. Right, hold still for a moment. I'll be able to examine her once she's out."

I felt the coldness of the metal tweezers against my ear and braced for the earworm extraction. I shouldn't have worried. Instead of the anticipated pain, a wave of peaceful calm spread over me. Sighing, I lay back against the pillow, enjoying the silence. It was like I'd been in a room full of electrical equipment buzzing and humming, a distant radio playing, the TV quietly chattering away in the background…and suddenly the power goes off. The absence of noise was a cool balm to my soul.

"Well, this is curious…I haven't seen one like this since the early trials. Which song did you say it was?"

"It has many, mainly eighties rock music, with a preference for David Bowie. At first it was a novelty, and quite fun to sing along with Journey and Simple Minds, but then it went on a glam rock medley for a couple of days, and that got rather annoying. I was constantly self-conscious about nodding along to songs like 'Tainted Love', or suddenly launching into the chorus of 'Love Shack'…." I tailed off, realising the doctor was staring open-mouthed, clearly baffled by my monologue. "It does have its favourites, but it has had a new playlist each day for the past two weeks. I guess this isn't one of yours then."

"Er, no, I don't believe she is one of ours. I may be wrong, but I think you've found a wild earworm. I've never seen anything quite like this. If I could breed from her…." Dr Squire carefully placed the precious earworm on a Petri dish and repositioned the magnifying glass for a better look.

"A wild earworm? Why…I mean where…er, how does one acquire a wild earworm?" I needed to know which places to avoid in the future.

"Well, that is the strange thing. They're incredibly rare in the wild nowadays, but for our breeding in the lab, they'd probably become extinct. I said they feed on earwax but it's actually the dead skin cells that make up their main diet...." The doctor became more animated with each explanation.

Ewww! Just my luck that a nearly extinct bug decides to take up residence in my ear.

"...So, wild earworms would have traditionally lived in dark, damp places where dust collects. But with the invention of vacuum cleaners and cleaning products, sadly their natural habitats have been sanitised," the doctor continued.

My mind strayed back to the old bookstore I'd browsed around a couple of weeks back. It was one of those stores with rickety shelves placed haphazardly, and old sofas full of mismatched cushions to entice customers to sit and read for a while. I remembered the unique smell of antique books mingled with damp dust and faint wafts of incense – the place probably hadn't seen a vacuum cleaner in years. The owner seemed oblivious to his customers, preferring instead to sing along to a dodgy eighties' mixtape, while reading from the huge pile of books on the counter. I made a mental note not to linger on the sofas again, should I ever go back.

Similarly, the doctor was lost in his own thoughts as he examined the earworm.

"Remarkable, quite remarkable...would it be possible...may I keep her?"

He doesn't seriously think I want to keep that thing, does he? "Yes, please do." I nodded vigorously and sidled nearer to the door. The doctor, overjoyed, turned his attention back to the earworm.

"Erm, Dr Squirrel, er Dr Squire?" I called; thankful he was too engrossed in the tiny wriggling blob sitting in the Petri dish to notice my slip. "Am I good to go now? All done?"

"Oh, yes. Sorry, I was rather distracted by this beautiful creature. Sorry, perhaps we should talk about the payment? Would ten be okay?"

"Ten?" *I knew I shouldn't have trusted that receptionist. Still, ten quid isn't much more than a prescription cost. It's worth a tenner to have some peace and quiet inside my own head.*

"Yes, of course, you're right – fifteen?" the doctor countered, "and thank you so much."

"Sorry, I thought there was no charge for this procedure, but yes, fifteen is fine. Thank you." I was truly thankful to get rid of the eighties' tinnitus playlist, and especially so now that I'd discovered what the actual problem was. I shuddered involuntarily. I didn't want to think about it any longer. I just wanted to pay the bill and get back to a normal, peaceful life. I saw myself out, leaving Dr Weirdo Squirrel singing along with my ex-earworm.

"Sorry, so rude of me," he called down the corridor. "If you wait at the front desk, my receptionist will sort out the payment. I shall ring through to her now. Thank you again. I am so grateful that you came in."

*****

The receptionist cheerily informed me she'd only take a moment to update my file and process the payment. I sat by the window, relishing my new-found ability to listen to everyday sounds without a rock guitar accompaniment.

"Excuse me, I'm ready for you now," chirped the cheery receptionist, and beamed over the desk. "If you could just sign here…and here…date here…thank you. Now, this is for you, I believe." She handed over a plain white envelope. I took it and handed over my credit card, but she brushed my hand away. "As I said earlier, there is no charge for this procedure. Dr Squire was most insistent and clear in his instructions."

*****

This was definitely the most surreal doctor's visit I'd ever had. I was still baffled by what I'd seen, but thankful to be back home, and without having any costs to deal with. Absentmindedly, I opened the envelope, ready to chuck the doctor's record sheet in my drawer of stuff to be filed, but stopped dead. Inside was a crisp cheque. *What the heck?* I took in the official surgery stamp, the illegible signature and today's date, but my brain couldn't compute the figure, as the zeros jumped around, refusing to be counted. *Fifteen thousand pounds! What the heck?*

With shaking fingers, I turned over the cheque, then flipped it back again. I wasn't mistaken. That creepy, wax-munching, noisy worm that had driven me insane for two weeks had solved all my money worries. It was like money for nothing.

Dammit! Now I've got a different kind of earworm!

Epilogue – a few years later

Dr Lynn did a last check that he had his notes in order, then strode onto the stage. It wasn't the first time he'd done a talk about earworms, but this was his first presentation on the latest upgrade – the Superworm! Not only was it the newest breakthrough in relieving tinnitus noise, it was also predicted to be the newest craze in the entertainment world. Dr Lynn had been quick to see the implications of the Superworm's ability to memorise hours and hours of music. And it wasn't just restricted to the music programmed into it at birth. No, the Superworm had the ability to learn as it grew. Couple that with it having a lifespan of only twelve months, there was a lucrative business ahead for regular upgrades – at a cost, of course.

The Royal Albert Hall in London was perhaps the most prestigious place he'd lectured at, but Dr Lynn needed a more theatrical venue. He had prepared his performance to suit a different audience than his usual colleagues. Gone were the days of dry lectures to stuffy old doctors. Now he had actors, singers, agents, and record producers clamouring to sponsor the latest trend in the music industry.

Dr Lynn started with a brief history of the earworm, finishing in assurances of how quick and safe it was to fit one. His assistant demonstrated this by fitting a Superworm into Dr Lynn's ear, live on stage. The crowd clapped at the simple procedure, but the applause ramped up when the assistant placed the microphone next to the doctor's ear. The voice of the tiny Superworm sang out the latest chart topper through the many speakers positioned around the theatre.

The doctor then sat down at the edge of the stage, while his assistant played a video to the excited crowd. He'd done his research and knew exactly which celebs and record companies would be attending. The earworms on the video had been strategically programmed to showcase the songs of the richest in attendance. As each of their songs were featured, the stars whooped and cheered. Some jumped up and sang along, while others quietly bowed to their peers.

It was going better than Dr Lynn had hoped for. He pictured the orders rolling in, his bills paid off, new house, flash car.... Distracted by his daydreams, he didn't realise at first that the Superworm was still singing. This demo model was only supposed to be programmed to sing one song, then stop, allowing him to demonstrate then continue the performance with a clear head.

On stage, the video was coming to an end and Dr Lynn's assistant was beckoning him to come back on. Confused, he realised his earworm was still singing, but there was nothing he could do about it now. Trying to ignore the tune in his head, he strode confidently back to the front of the stage and waved to his adoring audience.

Soon the talk was over, it was on to the after party – a meet and greet networking type event. Lynn really hated these things, but it was a necessary evil to get the new side of his business up and running. Distracted by the noise in his head, Dr Lynn struggled to smile and answer the many inane questions of the now drunk celebrities. Repeatedly, he looked for his assistant to remove the earworm, but the man was nowhere to be found.

*****

The following day's newspapers reported how Dr Lynn had suddenly gone crazy, grabbed a knife from the buffet table, and slashed and stabbed his way through a room of shocked celebrities. They described in detail, the carnage as blood splattered and dripped into the canapes, while panicked singers screamed and bolted for the exits. The papers went on to describe how the crazy doctor had then charged around London on a killing spree, repeatedly shouting, "No more, for the love of god, no more." The reporters went to great lengths to interview the traumatised actors, some of whom had barely sustained a scratch, but wanted to claim the limelight, and they gleefully played footage of the police swat team who finally brought him down in a hail of bullets. Yet nobody, not one single reporter could say why the good doctor had suddenly switched into a homicidal maniac.

*****

Back at the lab, Dr Squire, Dr Lynn's trusty assistant lovingly placed his Superworm into a vial and fed her some earwax. He'd managed to remove her from Lynn's ear before the coroner carted him away. Quickly, he switched on his MP3 player and placed it next to the vial. He couldn't risk her being used again while in her current state. He felt a little guilty about the deaths and the many who'd been injured during Lynn's bloody rampage. He'd only wanted to send the doctor a little crazy and discredit him enough to take over as the company director. He admitted to himself, he'd totally underestimated the effects of Rick Astley on a permanent loop.

The Magic Box of Apples

Magic can be found in all things.

Annie sighed and paused as she heard the tapping from the front door. Nobody used the front. Well, nobody who knew her…. Maybe there would be an occasional tap, just to let her know they were on their way round to the kitchen door, but nobody would expect to be let in the front. She listened for footsteps up the side path, but instead, the tapping became louder and more insistent. Sighing, she removed her apron, wafting clouds of flour away, then headed down the corridor. Front door callers were either unwanted or bad news.

"Excuse me, I don't mean to disturb you…but er…I think you've just been robbed."

The front door caller was a flustered young man, wearing only jeans and a scruffy t-shirt. He shivered in the chilly evening air as he faltered, wondering how to explain further. A gust of wood smoke-scented wind swirled around Annie, causing her to shiver too. The lad looked harmless enough; whatever was going on was better sorted out in the warmth of the kitchen.

"Well, you better come in out of the cold, love. T'is gonna be a chilly one tonight." Annie smiled and held the door wide.

The young man hesitated, looking torn between reluctance to get involved, and being polite.

"Come on, you're lettin' a draught in. I'll stick the kettle on, and you can explain all about it. I'm sorry, but you'll have to come sit in the kitchen. I'm just in the middle of baking."

Annie never tired of the smell of baking – scents of warm pastry and stewed apples, spiced with a hint of cinnamon and nutmeg, greeted them as she guided the young man to a chair. Annie checked the pies in the oven, adjusted the temperature, then filled the kettle. As she spooned coffee into mugs, she was aware that the lad watched her every move in silence. Finally, she joined him at the table with two steaming mugs and a plate of home baked oaty biscuits.

"OK then, so what makes you think I've been robbed? I've been here the whole time, and I've not seen a soul since lunchtime…apart from you, that is."

The lad warmed his hands around the mug. "I was walking back to my gran's – I've just come from the train station – and I saw someone go up to your porch. I didn't think much of it really, but then I saw them bend down and take something out of the wooden box. I watched them fill a bag with your stuff, then run off across the road. I'm so sorry, I should have shouted or stopped them, or something...."

Annie chuckled, then smiled at the lad's confused face. "Have a biscuit and drink your coffee before it goes cold. It's OK, I haven't been robbed. That would have been Jean picking up the chutney from the magic apple box."

The lad looked even more confused, took a bite of the biscuit, smiling. "Mmmm, these are good. Chutney?"

"Yep, five jars of apple chutney. Jean promised to deliver them to the school for the autumn fair – they're setting up the hall tonight. She was probably in a rush. Jean's always in a rush. Anyway, where are my manners? I'm Annie, but most folks call me Granny Apple around here...."

"Pete, Peter Aspen," he replied, and eyed the plate of biscuits.

"Go on, have another. They're freshly baked today. So, Peter, you said you were on the way to your gran's...if you're out without a coat, she can't be too far from here. Who's your gran?"

"Molly Howarth, from across the road," he said and took another bite.

Annie smiled. The lad's earlier reluctance and shyness seemed to be disappearing as fast as the biscuits. "Molly's grandson! I should have guessed. I can see the resemblance now." She watched as Peter brushed unruly curls of chestnut brown hair out of his eyes. "I remember the day your mum brought you round the village to show you off.

You were such a bonnie baby. But I thought Dorothy married some chap down in London. What are you doing back up north?"

"I've just started at the uni – it was my first day today. It was Mum's idea to stay with Gran. She thought it would do us both good, and the train stops not far from the uni. Getting the train in is a lot cheaper than renting in Manchester, and I suppose I can always stay over with mates if there's a party or something."

An apple-shaped timer suddenly beeped, cutting them off. Annie jumped up to silence the noise. "That'll be the pies ready, then. Do you want to give me a hand?"

"Sure," Peter replied. "What do you want me to do?"

"Grab those cooling trays off that top shelf and stick them down on the counter over there." Annie carefully lifted out two steaming pies – one large, one small – and placed them on the trays. "They need time to cool, but if you pop back after tea, I'll save a couple of slices for you and Molly. And come round the back next time. Now, talking of tea, I bet your gran has tea waiting and is eager to hear all about your first day at uni."

Peter promised he would pop back and thanked Annie as he left. She watched the lad dash across the road to Molly's and smiled. She suspected he would soon be back to sample the apple pies.

*****

"It's me again, Pete…" he called from outside the kitchen window. Annie ushered him in, eager to get the door closed—it'd soon be time to light the coal fire in the living room, she mused.

"Blimey, that was quick! Are you really that keen to sample some apple pie?" Annie chuckled as he settled back into the chair from earlier. "I'm just wrapping this big pie up for Elsie and Bob, over at number 8, then I'll cut a couple of slices for you to take back."

"Annie, you know before?" Pete asked.

"Ahem," Annie nodded back, and nudged the plate of biscuits his way.

"Well, you mentioned a magic apple box, and you said people call you Granny Apple…why is that? I asked Gran about it, but she said it was your story to tell."

"Your gran is right," Annie agreed. She moved the wrapped pie to the counter next to the door and then rummaged in a cupboard for a plate. "Yep, folks should be left to tell their own stories, and the magic apple box story belongs to this family. You see, I wasn't the original Granny Apple. No, that's a name that was passed down from my gran, to my mum, and now to me."

"And the magic box?" Pete interrupted.

"I'll come to that…. So, when I was a youngster, we used to visit my Granny Apple in this house every weekend. The house always smelled of cooking—if she wasn't baking pies and biscuits, she was making jams, jellies and chutneys, or some delicious pudding. It mainly included apples, though, on account of there being the village orchard just behind the house. Granny Apple was renowned for making the best apple crumbles in the whole county—or so she claimed."

Annie chuckled. "I loved it here. Granny Apple would teach me to cook and even shared her secret recipes."

Annie was interrupted by a tapping at the kitchen door. The visitor was just Elsie, picking up the pie for hers and Bob's tea. With quick pleasantries exchanged, Annie closed the door and cut the remaining pie into four. "There's a piece each for you and Molly, one for my supper, and one for lunch tomorrow—oh, I do love a slice of pie with a cup of tea. I'm looking forward to this."

Annie proceeded to transfer two slices onto a plate for Peter.

"But you still haven't told me about the magic box…."

"Ah yes…" Annie continued. "The box…. My granddad made that for my Granny Apple – it's made from apple wood from the orchard, you know. Originally, she used it to collect apples in, but as she got older, it was too heavy to carry, so she left it outside the front door. And that is when the magic started…."

Pete leant forward to listen. Yet again, they were interrupted by a tapping at the kitchen door.

"Granny Apple, sorry to bother you," the 'thief' from earlier stepped into the kitchen and closed the door behind her. "Oh, I'm sorry, I didn't realise you had company, Annie."

"That's OK, Jean. This is Pete – you remember Dorothy's boy, Little Petey? He's staying with Molly for a while," Annie explained. Pete blushed and gave a little wave.

"Of course! I saw you earlier when I was rushing off to the school—I thought you looked familiar." Jean smiled at Pete, then turned back to Annie. "Hope you don't think I'm being cheeky, but I just bumped into Elsie and the smell from that pie…. I don't suppose you have a couple of slices left?"

"Of course, you know Granny Apple always has a slice of pie for those who want one…."

"But Annie…." Pete started and quickly fell silent as Annie shushed him with a flap of her apron.

Annie handed over the plate with her own two slices of pie and saw Jean out of the door. "Now, where was I up to?"

"You were just about to tell me about the magic box, but what about your supper? What will you have now that you've given the last two slices to Jean?" Pete looked perplexed.

"Hush now, t'is just a slice of pie. I can have toast instead. And besides, my magic apple box will provide for me. That's how the magic works. But Molly will be waiting for her slice of pie. Why don't you pop back tomorrow and I'll finish the story?"

"But…." Pete, clearly intrigued, started to protest, but was once again shushed by a flapping of Granny Apple's apron.

"Now, the story will still be here tomorrow, and I have to get my beauty sleep." She chuckled, and her eyes twinkled with mischievous merriment. "On your way out, have a look at my magic apple box, then have another look tomorrow when you come back. I'll be making my famous gingerbread biscuits…."

The promise of more biscuits was enough to send Pete on his way. Annie had no doubt he'd be back for a tale and a biscuit (or three).

*****

"Hi Annie, I'm back!" Pete called through the window. Annie noticed he'd remembered a coat this time. It hadn't taken him long to get used to the chilly northern weather. He grinned as he handed the pie plate to Annie and took his chair at the kitchen table, glancing over to the biscuits cooling on the counter. The smell of warm gingerbread was intoxicating. It was enough to make your mouth water.

"So, did you look at my magic apple box last night?" Annie asked as she placed a few of the gingerbread biscuits onto a plate and filled the kettle.

"I did, but it didn't look that magic," he replied.

"Did you happen to look again when you came past the front door?" Annie asked.

"Yes, I stood and looked at it for a while, but the only thing different was that it was full of apples, plus there's a bag full of blackberries too. The box is just a box, isn't it?"

Annie chuckled again. She took her time pouring the kettle and making the coffee. Finally, she set the steaming cups and plate of biscuits down on the table and resumed the conversation.

"Oh, it's a box, that's for sure, but it is definitely magic. It all started when my Granny Apple placed it on the front porch. She emptied out the apples to make crumbles, but when she popped out to the shop for more sugar, it was full again. The next day was the same. She'd empty the box, then later that day, she'd find it laden with fruit. It started with a few apples, then as time went on, there would be pears, raspberries, blackberries…sometimes even vegetables."

"But how can that be?" Pete said, reaching for another gingerbread.

"Magic! Magic of the purest kind. And the magic box doesn't just fill with fruit and veg either. No, it provides whatever is needed. Some days it's sugar, other days a bag of flour, and sometimes there are jam jars. Whatever I'm running low on, my magic apple box provides."

"Wow! That's amazing. I'm not quite sure if I believe in magic, but if it's true, that would be pretty neat. Hey, do you think it could magic up a new laptop for me? I've been saving up for one for ages now." Pete looked thoughtful for a minute, then glanced at his watch and drained his coffee. "I'm sorry, but I need to rush off. I've got my first lot of homework and it'll take ages just to get Gran's old computer booted up."

"Of course, but could you do me a little favour before you go? Pop out front and bring me back whatever is in the box, will you?"

"Sure," said Pete, jumping up. He returned a minute later laden with fruit.

Annie handed him a box of gingerbreads to take home. "Just a little treat for when you've finished your work. Now, my magic box is empty. Be sure to check it again when you pass by tomorrow."

"I will, and thanks again for the biscuits," he called as he scurried out of the back door.

The following day, Annie was greeted by a, "Yoo hoo!" from the back door. She opened it and found Pete standing there, struggling to hold a pile of apples and a bag of flour, all balanced on a pie dish. "Look what I found!" he said with a grin. "It was empty last night, but it was full again as I came past. You sure you're not playing a joke on me?"

"No, no. I wouldn't do that," Annie said, catching a rolling bag of flour. "Put that down on the counter, love, before you drop everything. Shall I stick the kettle on?"

Pete grinned and took his usual seat. "Actually Annie, I have a favour to ask."

"OK, ask away…" Annie grinned over her shoulder as she busied herself making coffee.

"So, we have this project in uni, and we have to create a product with resources that are readily available, and then market it."

"Ooh, that all sounds a bit complicated to me, love. I'm not very technical."

"No, Annie, you'd be perfect. I was wondering if you could teach me to make a pie or something, then I can take photos of it and market it as if it was going in a posh shop."

"Oh, well, in that case, I'd be delighted to help. You don't have to be in uni on Saturday, do you? Why don't you come by tomorrow and we'll see what the magic box provides and go from there."

The two drank their coffee, and Pete explained his plans to Annie. From time to time, neighbours showed up at the back door to collect freshly baked apple crumbles and biscuits wrapped in napkins. Again, Pete queried why she worked so hard only to give her delicious baking away, but Annie just brushed it off, "Bah, there's far too much for me to eat. And besides, if I stopped baking, the magic box would stop filling."

*****

The next morning, Pete arrived bright and early, mildly embarrassed that his gran had insisted he wear her flowery apron. As expected, the magic box held just what he needed—a mound of apples, a bag of sugar, a wrap of butter and a bag of flour. It took him two trips to deliver everything to the kitchen counter. By the time Pete had balanced the last apple in the fruit bowl, Annie was ready with a coffee, and the now customary plate of biscuits—today's delicious treat was shortbread sprinkled with extra sugar.

While they nibbled biscuits and sipped the steaming coffee, Pete excitedly outlined his plan. He would first take photos of the ingredients, then a photo of Annie holding the finished pie. He already had ideas for the logo—Granny Apple's Magic Pie. He showed his sketches to Annie, and stressed that the final copies would be done on the computer and be much neater. Then, cups drained, and the last shortbread crumbs licked from their fingers, they were ready to start baking.

Pete snapped photos on his phone while Annie got out pans and pie dishes. Then it was over to Annie, and Pete was a willing apprentice. With a promise not to tell anyone the secret Granny Apple recipe, the two got to work.

There was enough pastry and apple mixture for several pies. "There's one for you, one for me, and the rest to share with whoever pops round first," Annie said as she closed the oven door. "I think we deserve another coffee after all that hard work."

"You sit down, Annie," Pete said kindly, and guided her to the chair. "This time, I'll make you a coffee."

*****

Annie was surprised that Pete didn't show up on Sunday. She'd grown quite used to his visits and missed having someone to natter to while she pottered around the kitchen. She was just about to lock up for the night when she heard footsteps thumping up the path. She opened the door wide to find Pete, brandishing a phone and a huge beaming smile.

"Annie, is it too late to come in?" Pete asked. "I desperately wanted to get this done so I could show you." He waved the phone again.

"You better come in then," she replied, giggling. "You only just caught me. I was locking up for bed."

Pete opened a file on his smart phone and flicked through the documents. One showed just the logo he'd designed, another showed a mock-up of a label, and others showed different adverts. Each one sported the Granny Apple logo and colour scheme, and the tag line – Handmade with fresh, local ingredients.

"Wow! It looks so professional. In fact, if I didn't make my own pies, I'd go out and buy these ones," Annie giggled.

"Do you think so?" Pete queried, but it was clear from his expression that he was secretly proud of his work. "I'm going to hand it in on Monday. I really want to get a distinction."

The next few days passed by pretty much the same as they had before the excitement of Pete's project. Pete would collect the stuff from the magic box and deliver it to Annie on his way to uni, then pop back in for a natter and a biscuit on his way home.

On Friday, Pete dropped a pile of apples off, then sped off to uni. Annie was used to his routine by now and already had a plate of his favourite gingerbreads ready. But Pete didn't show up. 'Maybe his train has been delayed,' Annie mused. An hour later, she put the gingerbreads back into the tin and locked up for an early night. She berated herself for relying on the young lad to keep her company. It was Friday night, and he'd probably be out with people his own age.

By Saturday coffee time, there was no sign of Pete, so Annie wandered round to the front to collect the contents of her magic box. She stood in front of the porch for a moment before it sunk in; the box was gone! In its place was a clean patch where the box had been, clearly visible against the weathered stone. She looked over to Molly's house, wondering if she should go check on Pete, but argued with herself that it was none of her business how the lad spent his time. Besides, she had the mystery of the missing box to solve—two mysteries, in fact, a missing box and a missing boy. Annie suspected the two were connected, but couldn't think how or why.

Sunday passed without event, and by teatime, Annie was both curious and a little worried by Pete's absence. She knew he had no obligation to visit; he wasn't even her grandson, but still, she felt they'd built up a friendship. If she was honest with herself, she felt quite hurt that he hadn't popped round, even if it was just to let her know he would be busy with uni work, or something. She hadn't worried like this since her own daughter was his age. 'A quick call to Molly won't hurt, will it?' she mused, but her hand was already dialling the number.

Molly's cryptic response was both a relief and perplexing. Pete was fine, though he had been busy, and had an explanation for Annie. Molly wouldn't be pushed when she probed for more information, insisting that it was Pete's tale to tell. She couldn't argue with that. Molly promised that he would be round as soon as he had finished what he was doing.

Annie had just finished cleaning up the kitchen when she heard familiar footsteps thumping down the path. She expected the usual, "Yoo hooo! It's me, Annie," but instead, there was a rather formal knock at the back door. Pete was flushed, his shoulders dropped, head hung low, so his mop of curly, brown curls hid his eyes. Annie was ready to tease him about abandoning her, but when she saw his sad face, she softened. She put her arm around his shoulders and guided him to his usual chair.

"I hear from your gran; you have a story to tell me. All stories are best told with a coffee and a biscuit. Why don't you start while I put the kettle on?"

Pete cleared his throat and mumbled about being sorry.

"What are you sorry for? I suspect it's to do with my missing box, but why don't you start at the beginning? Just tell your story, then we'll sort out whatever it is that has you so worried together."

"Well…I handed in the project. It looked amazing printed out, and I was the first to hand it in."

Molly was about to offer praise, but sensed the time wasn't right. She nodded and gave what she hoped looked like a proud smile.

"So, because I was the first to hand it in, the lecturer asked me to present it to the class. I was a bit nervous, and I waffle a bit when I'm nervous…like now." Pete blushed and continued, "Then people started asking questions, like, 'where did your inspiration come from?' I explained about the magic box of apples, and they all laughed at me. So, on Friday I borrowed the magic box so I could prove it to them, then they'd stop laughing at me."

Pete looked up at Annie, clearly struggling to go on, but was saved by the whistling of the kettle. The warmth of the coffee cup seemed to give him the strength to carry on. "I carried the magic box into the common room and set it up with some books in it. Then I took them out and made everybody leave while the magic worked…."

"But it didn't work, did it?" Annie said kindly. "Oh Pete, you daft lad! I suppose this is as much my fault, filling you full of tales of magic boxes. It is magic, but not in the sorcery-magic-spell kind of way. It works only on the magic of kindness."

"I get that now, but that's not the worst of it. So, at first, they just laughed at me, but now they think I'm a complete dork. One of the lads picked up the box pretending to be me, mimicking my voice asking for the magic to work. Then he laughed and dropped it. Oh Annie, I'm so sorry – it broke! I collected up the planks and came straight back to Gran's. I planned to mend it before I came round to explain and say sorry."

"Well, that's quite a tale. You know, you could have just popped in on your way home and told me. I wouldn't have been angry; in fact, I was a little worried about you." With the worst part of the tale over, Annie opened the tin of homemade biscuits and offered them to Pete. The buttery, crunchy oat cookies brought a smile to his face. "So, did you fix the box? I suspect that's not the end of the story, given that I haven't seen you all weekend."

"You're right. Gran didn't have the right tools, and a couple of the bottom planks were rotten at the edges. Gran suggested I go ask Bill down the lane for help, but on the way, I spotted Jean struggling to bring her shopping in. I helped her carry the bags from the car and she gave me a few spare planks she had in the shed that I could use for the box. I then went to Bill's, but he was busy tidying up his workshop. I swept up and tidied away his tools while he cut the new wood for the box. I told him about the project and showed him on my phone. He was really excited and suggested adding the Granny Apple logo to the box—he told me that his neighbour, Bert does pyrography as a hobby, and he would probably help."

"Wow, you have been busy," Annie chuckled, and offered another biscuit.

"But that's not the end of it. I went to Bert and explained my plans. He was just about to do a run to the shops, so I went shopping for him while he sketched out the design on the box. When I got back, his wife, Kay, insisted I stop for a cup of tea…I chatted with her for a while. Bert asked if I would leave it with him overnight and pick it up after lunch. When I went back, Kay gave me another surprise. I've left the box in its usual place. Will you come and look, Annie?"

Annie smiled and followed Pete round to the front door. The old magic apple box looked fresh and new again—chipped edges smoothed off, a fresh coat of varnish, and best of all, the fabulous Granny Apple logo was burned into the wood. Inside was a shiny package.

"That's for you, Annie. Go on, open it," Pete encouraged, handing her the parcel. His earlier sadness was replaced by boyish excitement.

Annie ripped open the paper to find a brand-new white apron, with the Granny Apple logo neatly embroidered on the front.

"Would you look at that! It's beautiful. I love it!" Annie cried and tied the apron around her ample waist.

"So, am I forgiven, then?" Pete asked.

"You were never in trouble, love. It seems the magic of the box has rubbed off on you. You see, the real magic comes from kindness and sharing. Baking is my thing, so I bake for my friends. I love doing it, and in return, the kids collect apples and other fruits from the orchard and leave them in the box. Jean picks me up a bag of flour every time she nips to the supermarket. Elsie recycles jars for jams and chutneys. Bill gives me a lift whenever I need to go anywhere…. It's a cycle of kindness that creates the magic. When I empty the box, it's quickly refilled with whatever I need, because folks round here appreciate a bit of home baking."

"I understand that now and I feel like such an idiot for showing off at uni. I knew you would appreciate me mending the box rather than buying a new one, but I couldn't do it on my own. I spent the weekend helping others, and now the box is better than before, and you have a cool new apron too..."

"Sorry for interrupting, Pete, but what's that in the bottom of the box?" Annie pointed to a flat, plain cardboard box. Pete knelt down to lift it out. Looking to Annie for confirmation, he opened the box to find a glossy, printed box inside. "What is it? I haven't got my reading glasses on."

"It's a laptop. Top of the range—exactly the same one I've been saving up for." Pete stared at it with a perplexed look on his face.

"I guess the magic apple box left it for you then," Annie smiled, but felt just as confused as Pete looked.

"It wasn't there when I brought the box round. How did it get there? It can't have been you, and I haven't told anyone else I wanted this one."

"Beats me, but my magic apple box does have a habit of providing exactly what is needed, and you need a laptop for uni. I guess the box has accepted you into our magic cycle of kindness."

"Perhaps it is real magic, after all...."

Hollin Hey

Flying the nest.

The farmhouse stood proudly on the hill overlooking the town below. Its white render glowed brightly against the dark fields that led to the moors beyond. It stood out from the landscape as now it stands out in my memory, a magical place of fun and laughter. Once a majestic manor, it had become a gently worn farmhouse, with 350 years of memories echoing round its walls.

Hollin Hey was more than just a home. It was a refuge for waifs and strays and a place of safety for the injured and unwanted. From the holly-lined driveway to the dry-stone walls, the garden was filled with a menagerie of mad animals. I'm not sure if they came with issues or whether they adapted to fit into our eclectic family, but each one had its own quirky personality.

It all started when my mum proclaimed, "What this garden needs is some chickens."

She had this idyllic dream of the gentle cooing of hens and collecting fresh eggs for breakfast. A trip to the local farmers' market started her dream, but instead of the brood of plump birds we were expecting, mum came home with the most pathetic, scrawny creatures I'd ever seen. What feathers remained were dull and caked in mud. They nestled together in the box, with more of a whimper than a coo.

"Nobody wanted them," Mum said sadly. "I felt sorry for the poor, little things."

They looked so forlorn, huddled in the corner of their new pen, shivering despite the warm sunshine. Within a week, though, they tentatively ventured out. The freedom to roam, good food and a dry hut soon had them resembling something like a chicken. As they grew in size, they grew in confidence and explored their new home with clucks of delight. It wasn't long before they'd established a sunbathing routine, scratched up the lawn, and designated the doorstep as a toilet, much to my dad's annoyance.

With the chickens settled in, Mum announced, "What this garden needs are a couple of geese to guard the place while we're at work." And so, it continued.

Mum's announcements became more frequent, and our dysfunctional family grew. Sam, the sheepdog with a fear of sheep, was next to bound into our lives. He claimed a sofa and discovered his vocation as a hen herder. A giant rabbit called Cally took over as 'top dog' and guarded the house with ferocious tenacity. Word spread locally of the strange people on the hill and their wonky collection of free-range misfits. Donations from well-meaning neighbours flooded in: injured and unwanted creatures, mad, lame or wild, none were turned away. Lawnmower-trimmed hedgehogs snuffled into the pile of sticks and leaves in the corner of the garden, embarrassed by their reverse Mohicans. They bedded down and hid away while their spines grew back. Ducks, chucks and pullets flocked in, wrecking the lawn with their dust bathing, and adding to the poop on the doorstep. Sam revelled in his new role and practised synchronised duck herding—the chickens had long since grown bored with this game and fluttered out of reach, mocking him. My dad was kept busy building huts to house each new resident to keep them warm, and safe from foxes during the night. During the day, they all roamed free, causing mayhem and mess. Mum's dream was becoming a reality, a noisy, messy reality, but we loved it.

We learnt quickly how to care for our growing brood. The injured were healed, the wild returned to their natural habitats, and the rest grew fat and content in their new home. Cally rabbit kept order well, and we settled into a routine. We started working with the local wildlife sanctuary, taking on animals and birds that needed release into the wild. Hollin Hey became a safe haven under the ever-watchful eye of a giant bunny.

The garden started to resemble Mum's dream as I started my final year of school. Lester the pot-bellied pig romped into our lives, creating havoc wherever he went. That pig had a great sense of humour and proved to be a better sheepdog than Sam. A pair of mischievous billy goats, Bruce and Max, were added to the mix, and we decided that was definitely enough. Actually, Dad said that after each new creature joined us. Mum never could resist a sad story though, and that was how our most challenging recruit came to us. A young crow who'd been reared in captivity, then kicked back into the wild appeared one autumn day. With his flight feathers clipped, he was unable to fly or defend himself, and had already been beaten up by the rowdy, local sparrows. The wildlife sanctuary told us of his sorry start in life and warned he was unlikely to survive. This earned him a place at Hollin Hey. We endeavoured to give him a fighting chance to reclaim his place in the wild.

Unlike the scaredy chickens, as we lifted the cardboard lid, he gave a triumphant 'Caw' and peered out defiantly. Jet-black eyes met mine and twinkled. I was sure I saw intelligence and mirth behind them. He fluttered forward to my outstretched hand, fell lopsided, but hopped back up and onto my finger. A silent moment of acceptance passed between us and for a second, I wished I could keep this marvellous creature as a pet. My reverie was broken by a sharp peck to the knuckles as my new friend tried to steal the shiny stone from my ring. Claws gouged grooves across my hand as I shuffled him gently back into the box. Maybe I'd have to rethink the tame pet idea.

"What shall we name him?" Mum asked. The big characters had been named, those who would be staying, but the wildlings remained just that. With our adopted naming system, this straggly crow should stay as crow, but something about him demanded a name. I stared into his coal eyes; he cocked his head to one side and regarded me quizzically.

"Ceefer!" Mum suddenly blurted out.

"C for crow," I giggled and Ceefer gave a loud 'Caw!' "Ceefer it is, then."

Ceefer was not impressed by being shut back in his box while we transported him to the abandoned barn over the wall. He shouted his annoyance all the way, claws scratching the cardboard as he tried to get out. The shoulder height hayloft was a perfect home, high enough to be safe from foxes and big enough for Ceefer to have freedom to recuperate. The ledge had a scattering of straw, sticks and old plant pots, all festooned with cobwebs and covered in dust. There were plenty of places for an inquisitive crow to explore and hide in. A grimy, cracked window let in just enough light to spark the dust motes disturbed by our entrance. He emerged from the box with a fluttering of wings and a disgruntled cry, scuttling off to explore his new home. We placed a bowl of puppy food and a shallow tray of water at the side of the ledge and retreated quietly. The light dimmed as I slowly pulled the door shut. Peeping through, I took one last look at Ceefer. He stood in the shadows, head cocked to one side watching, then he sidestepped into the sliver of light, nodded, and gave a loud 'Caw!' Maybe my fanciful nature was imposing human values on a wild bird, but it felt like gratitude coming from this tiny, fragile creature. Perhaps it was just relief to be out of the box. Whatever it was, I felt we'd made a connection.

"Goodbye Ceefer. I hope you like your new home."

As the first week went by, Ceefer grew accustomed to our presence. He'd rearranged the eight-foot square space, piling the straw and sticks in one corner and, annoyingly, he'd designated the water tray as a toilet area. 'Ah well, he'll get on well with the chickens', I thought as I rinsed the tray and added fresh water. Ceefer craved company. He soon learned our routine and would be waiting at the edge of his ledge, cawing with excitement. At first, I thought the food was the allure, but as soon as someone approached within hopping distance, he quickly scooted up an arm to sit on a shoulder. I'd learnt my lesson the hard way, and I had the scars to prove it. I now knew to take off any jewellery and wear a jacket, whatever the weather, to protect against sharp claws and brutal pecks.

There was intelligence behind Ceefer's jet eyes. He appeared to listen to everything and was a great audience for my ramblings. I absent-mindedly told him about my day and the antics of the other animals. He listened, head cocked, as I chatted about which chickens had roosted in Mum's favourite roses or how the pullets had escaped to the field. He pecked at the loose thread on my sleeve as I recounted the tale of how the pig had chased and terrorised the postman; the poor guy literally bolted across the yard and over the gate. Ceefer took it all in, watching as I filled his food bowl.

I arrived one day with a handful of mealworms, a favourite treat of Ceefer's. As usual, I called to him as I lifted the heavy iron catch of the barn door, but I was met with silence. I rushed in fearing the worst - cats, foxes, had a dog got in? I scattered the mealworms on the ledge, shouting to him. Nothing. Trying to avoid the spider webs, I moved the plant pots, hoping he wouldn't be there. Instead of the cold bundle of feathers I dreaded finding, I found a stash of treasure. I had no idea where Ceefer had found all this stuff, but hidden in the corner was a pile of teaspoons, nails, a broken earring, silver foil and bits of metal. My beady eyed crow had a love of all things shiny. Carefully, I replaced the pots to hide his treasure and called again.

A familiar scratching of claws came from somewhere out in the larger part of the barn, followed by an excited, 'Caw, caw, caw!' To my amazement, he fluttered down from the beams above and landed on my head. I giggled as he made his way down my outstretched arm. Ceefer dropped his most recent find onto my hand. A broken silver chain.

"Thank you, my friend," I said, attempting to stroke his head. My affection was met with a sharp peck to the knuckles. I shuffled him off my arm onto the ledge, but he fluttered straight back on. Like a proud mother, I watched him fluttering from the ledge to the beam and back to my shoulder.

"Now you're just showing off, Ceefer," I said as he cawed back triumphantly. His new wing feathers were starting to grow back. They didn't quite hold his weight enough for flying, but they gave him a new-found freedom to explore. My little friend had become a treasure hunter.

Mum and I discussed releasing Ceefer back into the wild with a mixture of excitement and sadness. Over the next few weeks, we scattered his food further away, hiding bits around the rubbish that had collected in the corners of the barn. Ceefer was forced to search and forage for his food. Each visit, we found an empty ledge, but within minutes, he would appear with an excited 'caw', bringing a shiny gift. My own collection of nails and teaspoons was growing as large as Ceefer's treasure pile.

"Right, my little friend," I said in response to his raspy call. "How would you like to meet the rest of the menagerie?" He hopped onto my shoulder and tucked his latest spoon down my collar. Wandering down the lane, I pointed out the field that led onto the moors and showed him the holly-lined driveway that gave the house its name. Finally, we came to the gate.

Ceefer shifted on my shoulder and nuzzled under my hair, a low, throaty rumble buzzing against my ear as he watched our dozy guard dog lumbering towards the gate woofing his welcome. Sam hadn't even noticed my shoulder companion and jumped up at the gate to be stroked. Ceefer peeked out from under my hair. Maybe it was the sunlight glinting off Sam's collar tag, or maybe just curiosity, but Ceefer hopped onto the surprised dog's back. Sam bolted into the garden, scattering basking chickens and lazy ducks. Ceefer rode the bucking sheepdog, intent on claiming the silver dog tag and apparently unaware of the commotion he was causing. Bruce and Max, already expert mischief makers, quickly joined in the game, leaping ducks and taunting Sam. I collapsed, giggling at the scene, unable to do anything productive.

Mum came scurrying out of the house to rescue the poor dog. With Ceefer on Mum's shoulder, Sam slunk off to his kennel. Cally rabbit herded the ducks back to the pond and calm resumed once more. It wasn't quite the visit I'd had in mind, but Ceefer didn't appear to be traumatised by his introduction to the rest of the gang.

Mum and I took turns to take Ceefer for walks each day. Some days we'd wander up the fields, accompanied by Sam, other days we'd potter along the hedgerows down the lane.

Ceefer's wing feathers were now fully grown back. He delighted in flying from shoulder to tree and back again. We gradually reduced his food until he was totally fending for himself. Ceefer was ready to go. He just didn't know it yet.

Towards the end of the summer, I was preoccupied with planning to leave home and go off to university. Mum took over walking the crow while I packed and planned. Finally, I could do no more. My belongings were packaged up and my childhood packed into a trunk in the corner of my bedroom.

My stomach churned with the excitement of new beginnings and the thought of leaving behind all that I'd known. I knew a walk in the fresh air would do me good. I collected Ceefer from the barn and slipped the broken silver keyring in my pocket, after retrieving it from down my top where the cheeky crow had shoved it. Mum and I set off up the hill in a companionable silence; even Ceefer seemed to sense the mood and wasn't chattering away. We reached the top of the hill where the fields bordered the moors. An old stone gatepost was the only thing to break up the landscape. Whatever the gate had led to had long since crumbled away, but the post remained, a mysterious remnant of the past.

I slumped down, back resting against the post as I caught my breath. Ceefer took flight, and I smiled as I watched him glide on the wind currents, then swoop down to the ground. I watched as he circled the trees that edged the field below. From here I could see my whole childhood world. Hollin Hey looked like a dolls' house with miniature animals roaming outside. Just a shiny speck of black floating on the wind, Ceefer did a circuit of the house, swooping down to the garden and back up to the roof. He glided down the holly-lined driveway and followed the trees back up the hill. Mum and I sat in silence as we watched him soar on new wings. He swooped and curled back up to the stone post where we sat. Automatically I held out my hand for him to land on, but instead, he fluttered just out of reach. Shiny black eyes met mine and with a loud 'Caw', he was off. With a mixture of pride and sadness, we watched as he disappeared over the treeline.

"He's not coming back this time, is he?" I said, not really needing an answer.

"No," said Mum. "And now it's time for my other baby to fly the nest."

Lilies For the Mantel

Echoes from the past linger on.

Dust motes sparkled in the sunbeams as he slid open the musty curtains. Wiping a clean spot on the grimy window, he stopped to peer out at the garden beyond. Smiling, he watched the children excitedly exploring the overgrown garden of their new house. The low swaying branches of the willow and a tangle of unruly rhododendrons made perfect hiding places for the two inquisitive rascals. The carefree laughter and squeals were a welcome backdrop to the arduous task ahead.

Where to start, though? The old farmhouse 'had potential', according to his wife. She could always see through the clutter and dust to the 'potential' beyond. Right now, she was busy, in her element, emptying boxes and arranging things; already creating a home in this dusty old building. He could hear her chattering away as she added colourful cushions and little trinkets to the drab, empty space. She'd already hung pictures on the old hooks, adding a little sparkle and charm with each addition. He had no doubt she'd create a comfortable, if a little eclectic, home for them in no time. He peeped in on her and found her pondering which fairy ornaments to put on the oak dresser. She held up two for his appraisal. They all looked the same to him and she would end up swapping them round countless times before she was satisfied, but nevertheless, he pointed to one. Happy, she turned to continue, and he wandered back to his chores.

Judging by the number of cobwebs, this room hadn't been used in a long, long time. Thick dust coated everything, but even the dust and cobwebs glistened in the sunshine, giving it a magical feel. Stifling a sneeze, he carried on sweeping and wiping away years of neglect. It was a wonky old place. The wooden floorboards creaked, the once white plaster walls were cracked in places and the ceiling beams were blackened from years of smoke from the open fire. It had a certain rustic charm to it. He imagined the room, clean and cosy, a rug at the fireplace for the children to sit on while they listened to a bedtime story. Then later, he would snuggle with his wife in front of a roaring fire. It was a nice dream but there was still a lot of hard work before he got there. Right now, the fire grate was rusty, and the mantel propped up in the corner. He concentrated his efforts on the fireplace, revealing a stone hearth under the layers of dust. Next on to the mantelpiece, it wouldn't take much to hang it. The old fixings would need replacing but he was handy enough.

The mantel was a heavy quality piece of timber; six feet of solid oak. He carefully lowered it to the freshly swept boards. Turning it over revealed a carved surface. Well, mostly. Intricate flowers in circular frames covered most of it; the last section was left rough and unfinished. Intrigued, he started to clean the grime from the ridges and furrows. The first was a rose set into a frame of thorny, entwined leaves. Exquisite detail, obviously hand carved; each petal and leaf now shone out. A wipe and a polish then revealed a simple daisy with a cloverleaf border; the next, daffodils, inside a ring of woven leaves. With every swipe of the duster, more flowers were revealed, some he didn't even recognise. Each one was different from the last, yet all had the same loving attention to detail. Someone had taken such care and time; he wondered what its story was.

Finally, he reached the last carving: not really a carving, just the outline of a lily with a border of heart-shaped leaves, roughly scored into the wood. He ran his fingers across the mantel, from the smooth polished rose to the rough unfinished lily. Nine flowers spanned the length of the mantel. Such a shame it was unfinished. He pondered whether he could finish it, but he knew his skills really weren't up to the job; he was handy, but not that handy.

He'd made good progress on the room, so he decided he'd have a break, a potter down to the village, maybe pick up some fixings for the mantel and check out the local pub. The children were still happy exploring and his wife had just unpacked a new box of fairies. They would be happier staying here. A quick check with his wife proved him right, so he set off, with instructions to pick up a bottle of wine for later.

The village was small but had one of those magical little shops that stock a random assortment of junk. Hidden amongst plastic bowls, gardening tools, pans and coils of washing line, he found a rack of fixtures and fittings.

Brackets bought, his next stop was the pub. You can tell a lot about somewhere by its pub, and this one was a quaint old place. It was an ancient black and white building with a tired but welcoming façade. There were benches outside, but it was just starting to get a little chilly to sit out, so he wandered inside, nodding to the locals on his way to the bar. The landlord served him with a cheerful greeting, and then went back to his chores, whistling to himself.

Pint in hand, he chose a seat next to the log fire. There was something so relaxing about staring into the flames, watching sparks fly and smoke swirl. The smell of wood smoke mingled with the old pub smell gave it a homely feeling. He took a long drink and sighed. Yes, this would do nicely. He planned to bring his wife here; the children could play on the green while they sat on the benches outside.

The old man in the chair at the other end of the fireside nodded and smiled. "You're a new face in here." He spoke softly, the wrinkles creasing up round his kind eyes as he smiled.

"Yes, we just moved into the farmhouse up the lane." He guessed it wouldn't be long before the whole village knew who they were. It was that kind of village.

"Know the place well. Used to live there with my Lily." The old man sat back and closed his eyes for a moment, a slight frown on his brow.

"We only moved in this weekend. I just popped out to get some bits to hang on the mantel. There's a lot of work to be done, but it's a beautiful house under all the dust."

The word mantel seemed to rouse the old man from his daydream. He opened his eyes and sat up straighter in his chair.

"Carved that myself, I did. Carved it for my Lily." He sighed, then sipped his pint. "She was the love of my life. Just wished I'd met her earlier. I was beginning to think there was no woman willing to take on a crotchety old fella like me, but my Lily was different. I knew we wouldn't have long together, but what time we had was special."

He sat back, pondering for a moment, remembering. A smile tweaked the corners of his mouth, and his eyes twinkled as he continued.

"It was Lily's idea to do the mantel. I carved her a rose for our first anniversary. Lily loved flowers; roses were the first thing she planted in the garden. That was her thing, gardening. She'd potter round weeding and planting and I'd sit on the bench carving, watching her. Each year, she had a new project in the garden; she enjoyed watching them bloom and by the time they'd died off, my carving would be done. A flower for every year we shared. She chose the wood for the mantel, you know, reckon she knew it would be long enough."

The old man closed his eyes again, lost in the past, his wrinkled smile growing. He seemed oblivious to the goodbyes as he relived his time with Lily.

The clock above the bar struck. It was time to go—just a quick stop for a bottle of wine, and then off to the farmhouse. The old man's story played on his mind on the walk back up the hill; so sad and yet so lovely. It was obvious they had been very much in love. He hadn't needed to ask about the unfinished carving of the lily. Some things were better left unsaid. The mantel must be hung, a part of the farm's history and a reminder of the permanence of love.

That evening, when the children were asleep, he recounted the old man's tale to his wife over a glass of wine. She was touched by the tale and urged him to finish the job; she was always a romantic soul. He promised he would first thing tomorrow. As she chatted about her day, an idea was starting to form in his head, now hazy with the wine. It would keep till morning.

The next day, the children were up early demanding breakfast so they could get back out to explore their new garden. He followed them out to look at their new den. Stepping across the daisy covered lawn, he noticed Lily's rosebushes hiding in the overgrown flowerbeds, the golden flowers attracting bees and butterflies. Up against the ivy-covered wall were terracotta pots of fragrant geraniums, almost hidden by the heavy pink hydrangea blooms. He hadn't really looked at the garden, just assessed it as an extension of the property compared to the estate agent's blurb. Now he picked out the flowers from the mantel carvings; delicate fuchsias, honeysuckle, and plants he didn't know the names of, had once been lovingly planted and tended to. He vowed to continue the good work in the garden, but now back to the house. He had a mantel to hang.

He enjoyed this kind of work; it was always good to see some reward for his endeavours. As he stood back to admire the new fireplace with the mantel hung proudly over the top, he remembered his idea from the previous evening. He would continue the old man's sentiment with a tribute of his own, but instead of carvings, he would paint. He wasn't an expert, but he had a good eye for colour and found it therapeutic. Lily had loved her flowers, but in his wife's case, fairies were an obvious subject for his canvases. He smiled as he pictured her choosing the perfect place to hang it. He would be required to stand holding it against the wall, while she stood back appraising. No doubt she would try every wall before deciding to hang it in the first place she tried.

No time like the present, he decided. He found the cardboard box that contained his pads and watercolours and carried it out to the garden bench. The sounds of his wife pottering about the kitchen floated through the window, blending with the squeals of the playing children. Colours of fuchsia and geranium pink, ivy green, golden rose, and lily white glistened as the sunshine bounced on his palette. His sable brush made a gentle stroke across the canvas as he started to paint the first of many tributes to his beautiful wife.

As he finished the painting, a carefree fairy with hair awry and a cheeky grin, he smiled at the likeness to his wife. She would love it, but his rumbling stomach reminded him of the time. He set the canvas down to dry in the sun, rounded up the children, and called for his wife. Today was a great day to go and sample the lunches at the local pub.

The lane down to the village was safe enough for the children to race ahead. They usually did double the journey, racing, chasing each other and doubling back. Today was no different; they splashed through puddles and veered off the road into the brambles and trees that ran alongside. The only indications of their progress were the big sticks that bounced above the tall ferns, occasionally whacking a low-hanging branch. The children were happy. This was definitely a good move. He sidled closer to his wife, taking her hand and drawing her close. She leaned into him, contented, and the comfortable silence between them spoke more than words could. He breathed in the fresh country air. You had to appreciate these little moments of calm when you were a parent.

"You're going to love the local pub," he broke the silence as they reached the end of the lane. They paused and waited for the children to emerge from the undergrowth. "It has benches outside, so we can sit out while it's nice. Let the children run off some of that energy on the green."

"Are they friendly? You know what country folk can be like with outsiders," she mused, not really believing anyone could dislike them.

"Well, I only spoke to the landlord and the old man, but they seemed nice enough. I've no doubt you'll have made friends with the whole village by the end of the week."

The children appeared, slightly dishevelled and still carrying sticks. He persuaded them to leave the sticks propped up against a tree to collect on the journey home. Spying swings and climbing frames on the green, the children raced off to play while his wife settled at one of the outdoor benches. Before he'd even got to the door, she was leaning across, introducing herself to a couple of a similar age.

The pub was busier than the previous evening. He looked around for the old man, thinking it would be good to tell him about the finished fireplace, but he was nowhere to be seen. The whistling landlord paused to take the food order and had time for a chat while he poured the drinks.

"I was looking for the old bloke who sits by the fireside," he asked him. "We've moved into his old home, the farmhouse on the hill. I wanted to tell him about what I've done with the old fireplace."

"Oh, you mean old Jim?" said the landlord. "That was Jim's seat you sat in last night. A sad affair that. When his wife passed, he kept smiling, then a few days later he went too, to be with Lily. My how time flies—I can't believe that was three years ago."

The landlord handed over the tray of drinks and whistled back down the bar, totally unaware of the impact of his words.

Dust motes sparkled in the sunshine as he pulled open the heavy wooden door. He stopped to peer out at the scene beyond. Smiling, he watched the children excitedly exploring the playground on the green—then slid into the seat next to his wife.

Penitence

Not all fairytales are stories

"Grandma, do you ever get lonely?" Jessica asked, putting a shiny goblet down on the table. She rubbed her aching arm—polishing the silver with Grandma was fun but hard work.

"No, love. I don't have time to get lonely in between your visits. I have many visitors stopping by for wishes."

"Wishes?" Jessica squinted at Grandma and grinned. This was probably going to turn into one of Grandma's weird and wonderful tales. They were fun when she was little, but now she wasn't so sure how true the stories of mischievous faeries were.

 Grandma held up the silver teapot she was polishing—she never let Jessica polish this one. It was too precious she'd explained many times over. Jessica could see that her grandma was pondering something. Her nose twitched when she was deep in thought, causing her glasses to slide down.

Grandma pushed her glasses back into place. "I think you're old enough to make a wish now. This is a magic teapot...".

"What, like I just rub the teapot and a genie pops out, saying, 'I grant you three wishes,'" Jessica said, giggling.

"Not quite a genie, but yes, that kind of thing," Grandma winked and placed the teapot in front of Jessica. "To make a wish, first blow into the spout, then say your wish out loud...but make it clear."

Jessica giggled again. Grandma was clearly getting lost in one of her old fairytales again, but it was fun to play along. She blew down the spout... "I wish for a large bowl of ice cream."

Jessica's reflection in the teapot's shiny surface shimmered and a wisp of blue smoke rose from the spout. She watched as the wisp rose to hover in front of her nose...it looked like...no it couldn't be... "Is that a faery?" she whispered.

The faery poked her on the nose, giggled, and darted out through the window, while Jessica stared transfixed, trying to process what she'd just witnessed. *So, all this time, Grandma's weird tales have been true...*

Grandma handed her the large bowl of ice cream that had just appeared on the table in front of them. "You wished for it! Here, eat this while I tell you about how I became the keeper of the faery jail..."

"Is this another one of your fairytales, Grandma?"

"It is, but now you've seen one, you know they're true. This tale starts a long time ago, when I was around your age….

"Back then, it was a simpler time. We didn't have televisions and mobile phones. When I got back from school and I'd finished my chores, my favourite thing was to climb up into the old oak tree outside your bedroom window. Then I'd curl up on a broad branch and read until I heard Mum, your great grandma, shout 'teatime'."

"I love that tree, too. It feels magical up there, like you're in your own private world, yet you can still see the house."

"Exactly! And it's more magical than you realise. Well, back then we had this old crazy lady who lived down the lane. Greta was harmless, really, and she would bake the most amazing biscuits. Most of the children avoided her because of the strange stories she told, but I quite liked her. I guess she was very much like I am now," Grandma chuckled.

"I'd often pop in to keep her company on my way home from school, and while I nibbled on freshly baked gingerbread or shortcakes, she would ramble on about the antics of the faeries who lived in the sycamore outside her house."

"She does sound just like you, Grandma," Jessica laughed, scooping up another spoonful of ice cream.

"Yes, and just like you and your brother, I loved the stories when I was little, but as I grew older, I stopped believing in them. I didn't want to offend Greta, though, so I carried on visiting her, and it was worth listening to a few crazy tales just to taste those biscuits. Greta kept her cottage spic and span; it was a lovely place to pass the time. There were always fresh flowers on the windowsill, unusual trinkets and ornaments adorned every shelf, and of course, it always smelled of fresh baking—whenever I bake biscuits now, that warm buttery smell takes me right back to my childhood."

"But Grandma, you were going to explain how you became the keeper of the faery jail, and I still don't really know what that is…" Jessica said, eager to discover whether this was just another one of Grandma's made-up tales. She was starting to wonder whether she'd imagined the 'faerie' shooting out of the teapot. Perhaps it had just been dust sparkling in the sunlight – that would make far more sense.

"Patience, Jessica, to understand what I'm going to share with you. You need to know how it came to be. Trust me, you will believe me when you know.

Okay, where was I? Ah yes, Greta's house was always so tidy, but one day I got there, and everything was chaos. Greta looked frazzled. Her normally neat hair was sticking out of her bun, drawers were open, trinkets knocked over, and there was flour everywhere! It looked like it had snowed flour across her kitchen."

Jessica giggled at the picture that formed in her mind, though in her picture, she saw a frazzled Grandma instead.

"I stared at the mess and gave poor Greta a hug—she looked like she needed one. Greta slumped down at the kitchen table, sending up clouds of flour, and started to cry. I didn't know what to do, so I did what my mum used to do when I was sad. I held her hand and said, 'tell me what happened. A problem shared is a problem halved.' Greta stopped crying and apologised for the mess."

"My mum says that too," Jessica interrupted. "Talking it through does help. So, what happened next?"

"How about we go get comfortable on the sofa and I'll tell you Greta's story. It'll be quicker that way, especially if you don't interrupt every few sentences, and you need to hear it all before I explain why I invited you to stay this weekend."

*****

Greta's Story

"It's the faeries," Greta explained. "A new family has moved into my tree and they're so mischievous, I can't keep up with their cruel pranks. And they keep hurting me too, stabbing me with pins, pulling my hair…it's just getting too much. My faeries can be fickle at times, but over the years, we've come to live in harmony. I leave out biscuits for them and keep the garden nice, and in turn, they use their magic to help with the chores, and they often bring me gifts." Greta gestured to the shelves of mismatched ornaments, shiny pebbles, and feathers.

"Of course, it took time to build up this relationship, but now we share a peaceful existence and I've grown to love my faerie neighbours—they keep me company and I think they enjoy mine too."

I listened to Greta. She seemed so sure of what she was telling me, and I was really wondering if she'd gone completely batty. But then something happened that shocked me, and I still remember, to this day….

There was a flicker of light, or at least that's what I thought it was, and something fluttered in from the window and landed on the table in front of us.

"Hilda, meet Soraia, the leader of my faerie friends. Soraia, meet Hilda. This is the little girl I was telling you about," Greta explained.

I stared in wonder at the tiny being; she was no bigger than a dragonfly and had the same iridescent wings. Her features showed a mixture of curiosity and concern as she stared back at me. I suddenly realised how rude I was being and held out my hand in greeting.

"Hello Soraia, nice to meet you. Please forgive me, but you are the first faerie I've met," I explained.

Soraia gently patted my finger with her minute hand. Her voice, when she replied, was no louder than a whisper, but I heard her words clearly.

"My child, I understand. We do not show ourselves to human folk unless we know we can trust them fully. My old friend Greta has assured me that you are worthy of our trust."

"I promise you can trust me, but why have you shown yourself to me?" I was still trying to get my head round the fact that Greta's stories had all been true.

Soraia smiled, then glanced round at the destruction and turned to Greta. "I see they've been tormenting you again. I'm so sorry, my friend. I will send over some helpers to put this right. They're causing just as much upset for our community too. I've been battling all morning to keep them from destroying everything we've built here. But now we must find a way to solve this problem once and for all."

"But can't you just use your magic to make them behave?" I asked.

"Sadly no," Soraia replied. "Faerie magic can do many things, but it can't change freewill. Any spell I could create to keep them in line, they could magic up a counter spell. They won't listen to reason, and they refuse to leave. It seems they were banished from their last home, and they're determined to take claim of ours."

"Hmmm, that's tricky. What about faery jail? Do faeries have a jail where they can send the bad ones?" I enquired.

"I wish it was so simple, Hilda," Greta added. "But Soraia and I have already discussed this. Neither faerie magic nor human spells could keep a faerie captive. They'd just create a new spell to escape."

"Exactly," Soraia said. "There is only one possible way, and that is to combine our magic to create a spell unbreakable by both our races. But even a single human cannot create a powerful spell like this, otherwise Greta would have helped us already. To create this combined magic, we need a human trinity, a maid, a mother, and a crone."

Greta picked up the explanation. "I know this seems strange to your young ears, but the old magic is still very much alive in some. I felt it in you when you started to visit me."

"Me? I'm not sure I can help. I can't do magic spells." I laughed because it seemed so ludicrous, but then again, I was talking to a real life faerie, and both Soraia and Greta appeared to believe in me. "Okay...," I faltered, "I'll try to help if I can, but what can I do? You'll need to teach me. And what did you mean by a trinity?"

"Perhaps I can explain our earth magic," Greta answered. "For the most powerful magic, we need three generations to symbolise the triple goddess: a maid—you, a mother, and a crone–me. The maid represents enchantments and new beginnings, exactly what we need to resolve the problem of our new neighbours. But the maid alone has neither the knowledge nor the experience to perform the magic. The mother represents stability and power, essential to bind with faerie magic. And finally, the crone brings wisdom, and in my case, the knowledge of the old magic."

"Greta speaks the truth," Soraia confirmed with a nod. "To combine your magic with ours is the only way to banish them from this place. I suspect that is how they came to be here."

"Okay, but I see two problems," I added. Despite the bizarre situation, I felt compelled to help, but had no idea how. "Firstly, we don't have a mother. We only have me and Greta. Secondly, if this kind of magic caused them to be banished from their last home, won't banishing them just move the problem somewhere else? I mean, what if they move into my oak tree?"

Soraia nodded once more. "You are wise for one so young. I think we need to rethink our plan."

"And if I may address your first problem," Greta added, "magic is inherited, and if I can feel it in you. I'm certain your mother has the gift, even if she's unaware of it."

"So, I need to bring my mother here to help too?" I wondered how I was going to explain this to her. She loved stories, but she was so matter of fact and practical. I'd need to get her here under a different pretence, but as soon as she saw Soraia, I was sure she'd want to help.

"Hilda, you mentioned earlier about a faery jail...," Soraia said, breaking me out of my musings. "This is not something we've ever contemplated before, but maybe it could be effective with our combined magic. Greta?"

"Yes!" Greta cried. "It could work. It would need to be silver to bind them. A silver prison, with a combined magic door to keep them from leaving, might just do it."

"That would work, but where can we get a silver prison?" Soraia asked.

I had already been pondering how to get my mother to Greta's house, and suddenly, I had an idea. "Leave that to me. I have just the thing. I need to go, but I'll be back after tea with my mother and your prison."

It was so difficult to keep quiet during tea, but as I helped my mother wash the pots, I finally had the chance to put my plan into action. I felt a little bad lying to her, but I knew as soon as she saw Soraia, she'd forgive my deception. I told her that Greta was going to teach me how to bake biscuits, but she'd need my mother's permission, given that I'd be spending the whole day there. Mother agreed to come with me and said I could go bake with Greta the following day, given that I had no school. Next was a tricky one, and I crossed my fingers, hoping that she would agree.

"Greta collects teapots, and I wondered if I could take our silver teapot to show her. I know she'd love to see it." It sounded a bit of a lame excuse, but surprisingly, Mother agreed. We set off as soon as the pots were put away, and I could barely contain my excitement.

Greta welcomed us in, and I saw immediately that Soraia had been true to her word. The kitchen was back to being tidy and there was no trace of the flour that had covered every surface. There was no trace of Soraia either.

As we sat down to drink tea, I placed the teapot next to Greta's cup, but the guilt of my lies weighed heavy.

"Mother, I must apologise. I wasn't entirely truthful about the reason you needed to come here. I'm so sorry, but when you hear the real reason, I'm sure you'll understand."

"Okay…" said Mother, looking far from okay. She had that polite smile she wore in public, but I knew it hid a wait-until-you-get-home glare.

"You see, Greta and Soraia need our help…"

"You know I'd happily help Greta; you didn't need to lie to get me here for that. And who is Soraia?" Mother said politely.

"I'm Soraia," the faery said, alighting on the table in much the same way as she'd done earlier. "And as you can see, I'm the reason Hilda gave you a more reasonable explanation for visiting."

Mother stared in disbelief, and I totally understood the confusion of thoughts going through her mind. "Mother, this is Soraia and she's the leader of the faeries who live in the tree outside. Now do you understand? If I'd come home talking of faeries and spells, you'd never have believed me."

"Shall we have tea and biscuits while we talk?" Greta said. "I know this is a lot to take in. You sip your tea and I'll do my best to explain."

By the time Greta had finished, Mother was looking less startled. She'd been studying Soraia the whole time, and I could tell she was going to help; her expression had changed to the one she wore when she was about to tackle a big job. She drained her tea and turned to Soraia. "So, it seems we have a problem to solve. When do we start?"

"So, we have our maid, mother and crone, and our prison, thanks to you," Soraia started.

"You mean my silver teapot? Hmmm, I guess that's fine," Mother agreed.

"Thank you," Soraia continued. "I will need to discuss this with the elders and devise the best spells for containment. Shall we meet here tomorrow at noon?"

"Agreed," Greta added. "I will also need to prepare."

Mother nodded her agreement, but I could see something was troubling her. "I understand you feel you have no option but to imprison these intruders, but for how long? And won't they just be angry once they're released and start again? Or worse, maybe? Is this going to put us at risk?"

"Very wise questions. I had not considered beyond removing the problem. I guess this will take more thought," Soraia agreed.

I'd been nibbling on a biscuit and listening to the grown-ups talk, but suddenly I had an idea. "When I've been naughty, Mother makes me sit on the step to reflect on my behaviour. I'm only allowed off when I say sorry and mean it – Mother can always tell!"

"That's true!" Mother chuckled. "I can see where you're going with this, Hilda. And if she leaves the step and misbehaves again, she goes straight back for longer."

"Exactly, but I'm not naughty that often now because I have learnt not to do the things that annoy you. What if you add a spell to the prison, which allows the naughty faeries to prove they've learnt their lesson?"

"I see," said Greta. "Only by using their magic for good can they be set free from the silver teapot?"

"So, I add a spell that can determine their intention…" Soraia added.

"Like, what if we asked the faeries to grant a wish, and if they did it nicely, they're free, but if they try to fool us by causing more mischief, the magic keeps them locked up?" I added. This seemed like the perfect solution, but it was also a fair way to give the faeries a chance to change.

*****

"And that is exactly what we did, Jessica. Well, Soraia and Greta did all the magical stuff. Mother and I were just required to join hands with Greta to strengthen and bind the spell. I'm still not entirely sure how it worked, but it did work. The troublemakers were trapped in my silver teapot the moment they started to play a cruel prank. Each time I visited Greta, we blew down the spout to wake them up and made a wish."

"And did they learn to behave?" Jessica asked.

"Not at first. It took weeks before the first one was released, and then that naughty faery was sent back to jail just a few days later. In time, though, their behaviour improved and everything calmed down."

"But Grandma, you still have faeries in the jail… do some never learn?"

"Oh, these are not the same ones, my love. But like children, there will always be good ones and naughty ones. I have six youngsters in there at the moment, the faery equivalent of rebellious teenagers," Grandma explained. "The original group did grow up to be respectful and fit in with the community and there was peace and order once more. In fact, when they had families of their own. It got a little cramped in Greta's sycamore, and some moved to live in our oak tree."

"Wow! That's why it feels so magical," Jessica said. "But wait, I thought you said faeries rarely show themselves to people. I saw that one who magicked my ice cream; what about the people who come for wishes, do they see them?"

Grandma chuckled. "No love, they think I'm a batty old witch and they mostly come for the entertainment. But you, my dear, come from a magical family. This teapot was passed down from crone to crone, from Greta to my mother, then to me. In time, I will pass it down to your mum, and next it will be your turn to be the keeper of the faery jail."

Vanished

A missing person and a Spanish adventure.

"Look, Scott! I can see the sea! The beach is gorgeous, and there's a little castle on the hill—is that the one you're going to be working at? I'd love to look round it. Shall we go? Oooh! Look at those little bars along the harbour…"

"Whoahhh! Slow down, Lana," Scott interrupted, laughing. "Yes, that's the castle, but I think it's closed at the moment. Look, I know you are excited, but can we just get to the hotel before you plan out the whole week?"

"Okay, it's just I haven't been to Spain since I was a child, and I want to see everything!"

Scott laughed again. "It's like sharing a taxi with a child with you babbling on. You haven't taken a breath since we left the airport. Right now, I just want to check in, then relax at the pool with a drink. We'll have plenty of time to see all the sights—we have two weeks to suss out the area, remember?"

"I know, you're right. I can't wait to get out of these clothes and put my shorts on—it's so hot here. I love it!"

"And I love that you love it," Scott said, giving me a hug.

The taxi slowed and took a right down onto the coast road. I could see our hotel not too far ahead; the sign, Vista al Mar was lit up in sapphire blue above a white marble and glass façade. It looked very grand. Little round bushes dotted with deep red flowers lined the impressive driveway. Excitement bubbled up. We were so close now, yet frustratingly stuck behind a coach unloading passengers. The taxi driver beeped his horn and shouted something out of the window. The coach driver shrugged and tapped his watch as he yelled back. *I really must make the effort to learn some Spanish,* I thought, but despite my lack of understanding, the meaning was clear—we were going to be stuck here for a while.

"Shall we get out? It's not far to walk, and we can easily wheel the cases down the path?" Scott suggested.

I agreed; it was too nice to be sitting in a stuffy taxi.

"You grab a case and go get in the queue to check us in while I pay for the taxi. I'll bring the bag and the other case," Scott said, already handing me my case from the boot.

Eagerly, I set off down the elegant path to reception. The double doors swooshed open, and I walked from the humid September heat into the cool of the air-conditioned lobby. It was just as magnificent as I'd imagined; beyond the front desk, patio doors opened out onto a pool, with palms and sun loungers dotted around the edges. Children splashed in the shallow end, while adults sunbathed or sat drinking cocktails. Bliss! This is just what we needed.

I mentally planned out the next couple of weeks. We would have to spend some of the time looking for an apartment, but that would be fun. There'd be plenty of time for cocktails round the pool and checking out the local bars. To the left of the front desk was a sign pointing to the restaurant, and another at the patio door pointing to the snack bar—my tummy rumbled at the thought of food. We'd been so lucky getting an all-inclusive holiday at this price, even given that it was out of season. *Snack bar as soon as we check in, then we can try the restaurant tonight,* I mused.

Finally, it was my turn to check in, but Scott hadn't appeared yet. I glanced back down the path, expecting to see him, but there were only porters waiting to unload the next coach load of holiday makers.

"Hello Ma'am, welcome to Vista al Mar, may I take your name please?" the receptionist spoke perfect English, that was a relief.

"Lana, er… Alana Meadows. We have a reservation for two, but I'm still waiting for my boyfriend to arrive – he's sorting out the taxi."

"We can wait a few minutes for him to arrive, or if you'd like, you can leave your bags here and look for him," the receptionist suggested.

"I'll wait if you don't mind. He won't be too long." I stood to one side to allow him to check in the next guest. There was no point in holding up the queue. Quickly, I logged into the hotel Wi-Fi and messaged Scott, but the message showed as undeliverable—of course he probably had no signal out on the road. I tried ringing, but it went straight to voicemail.

How long had I been here? It couldn't have taken more than three minutes to walk. I'd queued for another five, then a couple of minutes talking to the receptionist, and another five minutes waiting. I mentally added up the time while staring through the huge glass doors for any sign of Scott. Nothing. *Strange, he should be here by now. Surely he's not gone to the hotel next door by accident—that would certainly explain why he hasn't turned up.* I tried ringing again, but hung up as soon as the voicemail message started.

"Excuse me, sir," I said before the receptionist could start with the next guest. "Is there another entrance to the hotel? A different door, maybe?"

"No, Ma'am, this is the only customer entrance."

"Hmmm, he still hasn't arrived. I think I will leave my bag here and go look, if you don't mind."

The kind receptionist nodded, and shuffled my case behind the desk, while I tried to contact Scott again—still voicemail. I sent another text: *Where are you? I'm heading out to look for you. Ring as soon as you get this message.*

Back out in the midday heat, I strode back in the direction of where the taxi dropped us. The coach had gone, and so had the taxi, but there was no sign of Scott. *Perhaps the dozy idiot has tried to check in at the wrong hotel. They do all look similar,* I thought. It was worth a try. Another five minutes queuing yielded no results, the neighbouring hotel confirmed that they'd only checked in families, no single man in the wrong place. I was starting to get worried; my head was aching with running around in the heat. I desperately needed a drink and to get out of these clothes. I headed back to our hotel with a heavy heart. This was so unlike him. He even texted if he was going to be late home from work. There was no way he would just disappear without letting me know, especially if there was a problem.

It was the same receptionist when I finally arrived back at the hotel. He smiled kindly and handed me a cool bottle of water from the fridge behind the desk. I must have looked hot and flustered, I certainly felt it.

"Thank you, I think I will check in, then perhaps go back out to look for my boyfriend later. Is that okay? It's Alana Meadows and James Scott."

"Hmmm… James Scott? We have a booking here under the name of Alana Meadows – a single room – but nothing for a James Scott."

"No, that can't be right. I did the booking myself—a double room under both our names. Can you check again?" My cheeks flushed, and I could feel my heart pounding. This was not the idyllic start to the holiday I'd imagined.

"I'm certain, Ma'am. There's a note here that you phoned two weeks ago to change the booking to a single room. Are you sure you didn't forget, Ma'am? I mean, you are here alone?"

I know he was only trying to be helpful, but something in his tone pushed me over the edge. "No, I haven't forgotten, because I didn't change the booking. Don't you think I'd remember something like that? And no, I'm not here alone. I came with my boyfriend, who has mysteriously disappeared somewhere between the taxi and here. I'm tired, hot, hungry, and very worried. There's been a mistake. Check again."

I realised the people in the queue had gone quiet, listening in to my noisy outburst. I tried again with a more measured tone, "look, I'm sorry for getting angry but I'm just very concerned about my boyfriend. It's not like him to just disappear—something must have happened."

"I understand, Ma'am. How about we check you into this room for now so you can relax, and if he turns up, we'll see about changing rooms."

I could tell he was now questioning my sanity and just wanted me out of the way. "Okay, but I'll be back to sort out this mix up when he arrives."

The room was lovely, apart from only having a single bed. I would have been so happy with the sea view window and the small balcony overlooking the pool, had it not been for the circumstances that landed me here. It was clean, smelled fresh, and the bed looked comfy. Exhaustion was taking over, but the need for food outweighed my need to snooze. Apart from the bottle of water the receptionist had given me, I'd had nothing to eat or drink since the box meal on the plane. I decided to have a quick shower, get changed, and head down to the snack bar.

The shower did little to rejuvenate me, but the frustration kicked in again when I realised that Scott had the bag with our sun cream and toiletries. *Damnit! He's got our Euros and passports in that bag too!* Thankfully, I had my clothes, and I had my credit card in my handbag that would do for emergencies. Thank goodness we'd booked an all-inclusive. At least I wouldn't be worrying about food and drinks until Scott appeared.

At the snack bar, I ordered a burger and fries, then settled down at the poolside. For the millionth time, I checked my phone for a reply from Scott, but my message was still showing as undelivered.

"Hi, I don't mean to interrupt you, but I saw you at the check in… you look like you could do with a friend."

I turned to see a woman around my age smiling from under a giant sunhat.

"Hi, er…I don't think I'd be good company right now," I faltered. I just needed to eat something, then get back out to search for Scott. Once he was here, I could relax and socialise, but right now I couldn't even think straight.

"That's okay. It's just I heard what you said back there, and wondered if I could help. I mean, I'm here on my own… nothing better to do. I'm Amy."

"Oh god! You heard my little rant at that nice guy? I must have looked like a crazy woman. I'm Alana. I'm not sure how you can help, but I appreciate the offer."

Amy smiled and wandered away. I went back to checking the phone again—no luck there. *Maybe his battery is dead*, I thought, but it was unlikely, plus he had the portable chargers in his bag. I checked my battery—32%—that was another thing I would have to sort. If my phone died, I'd have no way of contacting Scott when he did have the signal to reply.

"Here," Amy appeared again and handed me a cocktail, "I figured you needed this. So, I overheard you've lost your husband…"

"My boyfriend—Scott." I corrected and sipped the sweet drink. Amy was right. It did help.

"So, I've been here a week already and I know the area. Shall we make a plan, and see if we can find your boyfriend?" Amy said cheerfully.

"Well, that would be helpful, but I don't want to spoil your holiday with my troubles…"

"Nonsense! You'd be doing me a favour. It was quite liberating being here alone for the first week, but there's only so many times you can get chatted up by drunken Brits before it gets tiresome. It'd be a breath of fresh air to have some female company—all the people here are either in couples or families."

"Well, if you're sure…" I agreed. The thought of having at least one friendly person helping gave me some reassurance.

"Ok, finish that and I'll get us another drink while we plan."

Amy soon appeared with the drinks, and by the time I'd finished my second strawberry daiquiri, we had a list:

Check hotel CCTV.

Check with taxi firm.

Go to the local shop for toiletries and a phone charger.

Check out local bars and restaurants.

If not turned up by tomorrow, make a police report.

I felt a little better once we had a plan in place, and together we headed back to reception. Thankfully, it was a different guy. He seemed bemused by my requests but agreed to check the CCTV. Unfortunately, it only covered as far as the hotel grounds—we could just see passengers getting off the coach that had blocked the taxi, but there was no sign of Scott, even when the coach drove off.

Next, we asked him if he could ring the taxi office at the airport. A few minutes of rapid Spanish, and he turned to us, shaking his head. The taxis outside were all private hires, and there was no way they could determine which one we'd used.

"Don't worry, Hun," Amy said. "We still have lots of things we can try."

"He's been gone over two hours now. Where can he be?"

"Leave your number with reception, in case he shows up. I'm taking you shopping. We can check the bars on the way. Come on, I know you're worried, but it's not going to help find him if you sit here brooding."

Amy was right. I needed to stay positive and be proactive. I discussed with Amy about going straight to the police, but they probably wouldn't take me seriously after just a couple of hours.

"Okay, let's go. And thank you again for being so supportive. I don't know what I would have done if you hadn't …"

"Eavesdropped and interfered?" Amy said with a laugh. "Right, shopping therapy, with some detective work along the way."

Luckily, I had a recent photo of Scott on my phone to show around the bars and at the shop, but nobody had seen him.

By the time we got back to the hotel, I was exhausted and dejected, and my phone had finally died. But for Amy's incessant cheerfulness, and also my lack of passport, I think I would have given up and gone home.

"Don't worry, Hun, go plug your phone in and get changed. I'll meet you in the restaurant in half an hour."

"Thanks, Amy. I'll see you in a bit."

I headed back to my room, but on seeing the single bed, I started to cry. Nothing added up. Scott had been just as excited about this holiday as I had. Then there was the strange mistake on the hotel system. *How can someone just disappear?* I wondered for the millionth time. I needed to get myself together. Another quick shower and fresh clothes, and I felt a little better. My phone wasn't fully charged, but I stuck it in my bag and headed to the restaurant.

Amy was already there and waved from a table over by the window. The restaurant was a buffet style, self-service, and it had such a variety of dishes to choose from. *Scott would love this,* I thought ruefully, but I put on a big smile and waved back at Amy.

We discussed the next steps while we ate. Amy wanted to check out the cafés along the beach the following day. That is, if he hadn't already turned up. Plans made, our chat turned more social, and I discovered that Amy was a nurse, recently divorced, and this was her first holiday as a single person.

"So, enough about me. Tell me about Scott. Maybe if I know more about him, it might help," Amy urged.

"Where do I start? Er… we've been living together for six years. He's an artist, well, actually he's a fine art restoration artist. His company covers a lot of different restoration projects, but Scott heads up the historic collections and interiors." I explained.

"Wow, that sounds like a cool job. He must be very talented."

"Yes, that's why we're here. Scott's company has offices throughout Europe. There's one in Spain, but he's kinda the expert, so he landed the contract to restore that castle on the hill. We're here on holiday, but we're also going to look for an apartment—it'll be a six-month project, so we figured it would be fun to live out here."

"And you're going to move with him? Oh, I'm so jealous!" Amy gushed.

"Well, I work from home, so it doesn't really matter where I live, providing I have my laptop and Wi-Fi," I explained.

Chatting with Amy was easy, and I almost put my worries aside. Then I heard the familiar beep coming from my bag. Quickly, I opened up the text and stared in stunned silence.

"What is it? Alana, Hun, you've gone pale. Is it from Scott? Is he okay?" Amy's voice switched from her usual jovial tone to one of concern.

"It's Scott…I just don't believe it. Something is not right…I need to ring him." I grabbed the phone and bolted out of the restaurant to find a quiet space, my cheeks flushed and my heart pounded With shaking hands, I pressed the call button. Nothing! Not even a voicemail message, just the out of service tone. Sadly, I wandered back to the table, where Amy sat with a concerned look on her face.

"Was it Scott? What did he say?"

"I didn't get to speak to him. I think the phone was switched off straight after the text. I just don't get it...look!" I opened the text and handed the phone to Amy.

Alana this is just not working out. i didn't know how too tell you before, but ive found someone else and i realised that i couldn't bear to spend a holiday with you. i'll be staying in Spain so youll have plenty off time to find a new flat and move your stuff out before I get back

James

Reading the text again, I burst into tears. Amy jumped up and gave me a hug, which caused another flurry of sobs.

"Come on, Hun. Let's get you out of here. Come back to my room. I have a bottle of brandy and you look like you need something stronger than these cocktails."

I let Amy lead me back, not really noticing where we were going. I just couldn't process the text. How could I not have seen the signs? How could he let me come all the way here, leave me panicking for a day, then dump me with a text? Nothing felt right. It just wasn't like Scott at all.

"Here, drink this! Calm your nerves, drown your sorrows—whatever, it'll help."

I suddenly registered that I was sitting on Amy's bed, and she was handing me a large glass of brandy. I downed half the glass, then slumped back to sip the rest.

"I'm so sorry, Hun, but at least we now know why he disappeared. This really sucks…" Amy started.

"I know how it looks, but something feels off. That text… I'm sure that's not Scott. Wait, let me read it again."

I checked the text and showed it to Amy once more.

"See! He calls me Alana in the text, but Scott's always shortened it to Lana, like his pet name for me. And he's signed it James…"

"Yeah, I did wonder about that. You've always called him Scott," Amy interrupted.

"His name is James Scott, but when I first met him, I was slightly drunk and kept calling him Scott. He found it amusing and didn't correct me. I even saved his number as Scott James. I felt a bit dozy when he finally told me, but the nickname Scott stuck. And anyway, who signs their name on a text? Scott never does."

"Hmmm…that does seem odd, but maybe he was just being formal because it was a breakup text. I don't know, Hun; men are strange."

"But, Amy, it's not just the names. There are mistakes in the message—wrong spellings and missing punctuation…"

"Autocorrect maybe?" Amy suggested.

"No, Scott is a stickler for correct spelling and grammar. He types slowly with one finger, and always corrects any accidental mistakes—I am always ribbing him for it. I don't believe this came from Scott."

"Okaaaay..." Amy drew out the word, clearly trying to decide what was true. "Let's say this isn't Scott, then who sent it and why?"

"I have absolutely no idea, but he's still missing, and I need to find out what's going on. We'll go to the police first thing tomorrow."

"Sweetheart, I know you know it isn't Scott, but if you go to the police with that text, they're going to assume you've been dumped by a lowlife. They're not going to take it seriously. I don't know what the missing persons procedure is in Spain, but I guess it will be similar to home. Let's do some more detective work tomorrow, then if we uncover anything, we can go to the police with the information."

"You're right," I nodded sadly to Amy, "thanks for everything today, but I think I'm going to get some sleep. I need time to process everything, and I'm just so weary with it all."

"Okay, should I meet you at the restaurant for breakfast?" Amy asked.

"Sure, that would be great. 9am? Goodnight and thanks again."

Amy gave me a long hug before directing me towards my room. Thankfully, we were on the same floor, so I didn't have far to go.

I awoke to bright sunlight flooding in through the window. In my exhausted state last night, I hadn't even closed the curtains. And I'd crashed out still wearing my makeup. My eyes felt itchy from the dried tears mixed with mascara. I hadn't looked in the mirror, but I suspected that I looked a mess. The clock on my phone showed it was 7.30 a.m. Too early for breakfast, but plenty of time for a long shower.

Amy was already there when I arrived at the restaurant, her smile beaming from the same window seat we'd been in the day before. I selected a plateful of fruit, cheese, and fresh bread, poured myself a large coffee and wandered over.

"Morning, Hun! How are you feeling today?" Amy's cheerfulness had returned, and it boosted my low mood.

"Better, thanks. I crashed out last night. I don't even remember getting into bed," I replied.

"Well, I'm not surprised, Hun. You had a helluva day yesterday. But today, hopefully we'll find some answers. And perhaps have a little fun along the way."

Over breakfast, Amy outlined her plan. We would head the other way, down the coast, and pop into each café and hotel with the picture of Scott. I added that we should try to ring his number every half an hour, in the hope his phone was switched on.

An hour later, we met in the foyer, sun hats on and sun cream applied. It was sunny out, but thankfully not as hot as July and August. We chatted amiably in between popping into hotels and cafés, and stopped occasionally for a cool drink or snack. Despite our efforts, nobody had seen or heard of Scott, and his phone was still switched off. We'd walked quite far down the coast, and we were both getting tired.

"Let's just do that snack bar and the beach bar, then we'll get the bus back," Amy suggested.

I grabbed a table outside while Amy popped inside to get us some drinks. I stared out onto the beach road, looking at how far we'd come. A bus ambled to a stop, and a mixture of tourists and locals poured out. *Thank goodness for the bus. I don't think I could walk back in this heat,* I pondered, then suddenly stared in surprise. The woman stepping off the bus looked familiar. I struggled to place where I knew her from, then it clicked—she was from Scott's office. I'd seen her a couple of times when I met him after work. Clara, Candy? No, Cassie. Cassie Green, that was it.

"Here's your drink, Hun…" Amy appeared with two iced colas.

"Don't look back, but there's a woman behind you—blue sundress—just got off the bus. She's from Scott's office. Don't you think that's too much of a coincid…oh god she's heading over here. What should I do?"

"Quick, go hide in the bathroom. I'll see if I can engage her in conversation, see what I can find out. I'll come get you when she's gone."

I couldn't think straight. I just followed Amy's instructions. Hiding in the loo, my mind ran through the many possible scenarios. *Maybe she's here on business, but surely Scott would have mentioned it, and why would she be here now? Perhaps just a coincidence that she'd decided to come on holiday to the same place, at the same time—unlikely, but possible.* The one thought I didn't want to torture myself with was that Cassie was here to meet Scott, and the text was true. *Could he really have been having an affair with her?* I sought through our past conversations. There'd been nothing of any consequence. According to Scott, she was a new secretary…*ah, that's it. Scott said he'd been having problems with her, but her contract was only temporary. He'd said it wasn't worth making a fuss because she'd be gone by the time we returned from Spain—'that's if we ever come back!' he'd joked.*

I felt the anger bubbling up inside me. I needed to confront her; I needed answers, and I needed to hear them from Scott, face to face. No more skulking in the loo! I strode out and nearly bumped into Amy.

"Whoah there, Speedy! She's gone, and have I got a tale to tell you!" Amy said with relish. "Shall we get the bus and I'll fill you in on the way home?"

We sat together at the back of the bus. Amy waited for everyone to settle down into their seats, then relayed the conversation.

"So, she, Cassie, wandered over, looking for a seat and I offered for her to join me, given that the other tables were taken. I made up a story about meeting my friend, but she'd just texted to cancel, and I gave Cassie your drink—sorry!"

"So, what did you find out?" I interrupted.

"The 'delightful' Cassie is apparently a restoration artist, specialising in historical buildings, and she's here to check out the area before her new job starts."

"Ooh, the lying little cow! She's a temp secretary, and not a very good one at that, according to Scott. Sorry, go on."

"I asked if she was here with her husband or boyfriend and she said no, but she was hopeful her boyfriend would move out to join her. She said they still had a few logistical problems to sort. I told her he sounded nice and asked if she had a photo of him." Amy paused for effect.

"And…?"

"She showed me this picture of what looked like an office group shot, pointed to your Scott, and said, 'this is my James.' Can you believe it?"

I listened, stunned, while I tried to process the information.

"There's more. I asked how long they'd been together… 'we've been living together for five years,'" Amy said, mimicking the sickly-sweet voice I remembered from our last meeting.

I laughed, incredulous.

"Hang on, there's still more," Amy continued in the same whiny voice, 'Bless him, he's only the admin assistant, but I love him, and he's so proud of me landing this big contract.'"

"Pah!" I spat out. "She's clearly delusional, and it's too much of a coincidence that she's here just as Scott disappears."

"My thoughts exactly!" Amy agreed. "Even with what little you've told me; I could tell she was lying the whole time. But it is quite suspicious, don't you think?"

"Exactly! We need to follow her…"

"I'm ahead of you there, Hun," Amy laughed. "I watched her go into that little hotel, next to the snack bar, and she had her key on the table, next to her phone. It had one of those big wooden tags on it—room 63," Amy finished triumphantly.

"You are so wasted as a nurse, my friend," I said, giggling. "Have you considered a job as a detective? Oh look, this is our stop. Let's continue this over dinner, shall we?"

I arrived at the restaurant first this time and secured our usual table. Amy appeared after a few minutes, and it wasn't long before we'd grabbed plates of food and settled back at the table.

"So, I was thinking," I started, "Why don't we have an early breakfast, then get the bus straight down to the far end of the beach?"

"Good plan!" Amy agreed. "And if she's there, we can confront her, and if not, maybe we can check out her room."

"And how do we do that?" I didn't really fancy being arrested for breaking and entering.

"I don't know yet. Let's just see what happens tomorrow. I'll have a think tonight."

"Of the many things that have been puzzling me… there are three possible scenarios: number 1, Scott's a lying scumbag who has been having an affair for five years, and he's with her voluntarily…" I started.

"But we don't believe that, do we?" Amy interrupted.

"No, but I'm considering all possibilities. Number 2, I can't work out how, but he's with her against his will, and for some reason, he can't contact me or get away."

"That sounds plausible," Amy agreed. "But how would she manage to keep him there? Do you think she has him locked up in the hotel room?"

"I just don't know, but there's a third option: Cassie is genuinely here on business, though obviously not for the reasons she bragged about. I don't know. Maybe she's here to sort out the paperwork at the Spanish office?"

Amy pondered it. "Possible, but if that is the case, then where is Scott?"

"Maybe something happened, like an accident and he's in a hospital somewhere unconscious…" I suggested.

"No, that wouldn't work because that doesn't explain the text you received," Amy added. "I think we have to work on the assumption that scenario 2 is the most likely. Now we just have to find him."

It was baffling, but with Amy's help, I felt closer to discovering the truth. We decided to forget about it for the night and went down to the bar. I hadn't relaxed since I got here, and we both needed to unwind.

The following day, Amy and I arrived at the restaurant together and ate a hurried breakfast. With a mixture of excitement and apprehension, we got the local bus down the coast. It didn't take long to reach the stop outside the snack bar. We'd decided to have a coffee and scope out the hotel while we built up the courage to confront Cassie.

It didn't quite go to plan though. As we got off, I saw Cassie jump onto the bus heading in the opposite direction. Thankfully, she didn't see us. I enquired with the driver about where the other bus went, and he explained that it went over the hill, to the next town.

"Okay, plan B?" Amy suggested. "With the bitch gone, we could go snoop in the hotel."

"Okay then, let's go! Er…did you come up with a plan for getting in?" I asked.

"I figured we'd just wing it and see what happens." Amy giggled, linking arms, and guiding me towards the hotel.

It isn't nearly as posh as our hotel, I thought smugly as we entered the small budget hotel. There was just one girl on the front desk, trying to deal with a bunch of rowdy teenagers. Cassie was a similar height and build to me, with a similar style of dark hair. I slipped on my sunglasses. They made a poor disguise, but I figured a flustered receptionist wouldn't notice.

"I'm about to wing it! Play along, Amy," I whispered and strode up to the desk. I waved to the receptionist, then adopting Cassie's sickly-sweet tone, I started: "Oh hi, sorry to be a bother. I've left my purse in my room and my friend has my key. Could I possibly use the spare key? Cassandra Green, room 63."

The teenagers continued to argue, and the poor girl looked flustered. She quickly tapped on the keyboard and glanced at the screen, then reached back and grabbed a key from the hooks behind the desk.

"Here, but please return it. Any lost keys will be charged to the room."

I said my thanks, but she'd already turned back to deal with the teenager situation.

"Great winging there, Hun!" Amy said, chuckling. "Couldn't have done it better myself."

Thankfully, there were signs next to the lift showing room numbers. Room 63 was on the second floor. Exiting the lift, I could feel my heart thumping. I wasn't sure what we were about to discover, but I hoped Scott would be there. The corridor was empty. We quickly sneaked into the room and quietly closed the door behind us.

It was empty. The bed was made, and the towels in the bathroom were folded neatly. It looked like the maid had already been round—at least we didn't have to worry about that.

"Okay, detective, let's hunt for clues," Amy whispered, opening a drawer. There wasn't much else in the room, just a kettle and cup on the dressing table, with coffee sachets and milk cartons neatly arranged in a pot, a chest of drawers and a wardrobe. The bathroom was small, with just a toilet, sink, shower, and a few toiletries scattered about. Amy was checking the drawers, so I opened the wardrobe. It was all as expected, except for the case and the bag shoved right at the back, behind what I assumed was Cassie's case.

"Amy, come look at this!" I said triumphantly, forgetting to whisper. I dragged the bag and case out and pushed her case back into place—hopefully Cassie wouldn't notice. A quick check of the bag revealed everything was still there, including Scott's phone, our passports, and the cardboard wallet of Euros.

"Well, well, well! Cassie has been a naughty girl, as well as being a liar. I think we can confirm that our scenario 2 is the correct one."

"I think so, but we still have no idea where Scott is. I was really hoping we'd find him here. Did you find anything useful?" I asked.

"Nope, other than the bitch wears very lacy knickers," Amy laughed. "Come on, let's grab the bags and get out of here."

I didn't need any persuading. As quietly as we could, we locked the door behind us and breathed a sigh of relief.

"Cassie, is that you?"

A woman emerged from the lift across the hall, startling us. I froze, not knowing what to say. Even though the bags were mine, I felt like I'd just stolen them from the room.

"No, I was just popping by to see if she fancied joining us for lunch," Amy said quickly. "We met yesterday, got chatting, and I thought it might be nice to catch up. Do you know where Cassie is?"

"Ah, okay, I'm in the room next door. I guess she'll be up at the castle. She has a job there, painting or something," the lady said.

I recovered my composure. "Any idea what time she finishes? Perhaps we can have dinner together instead?"

"I'm not sure exactly, but I usually see her between 4 and 5. Should I tell her you called?"

"No, it's okay, thanks. I'm sure I'll bump into her again soon, then we can arrange it properly," Amy said, smiling sweetly.

"Nice to meet you," I called after the lady as we headed for the lift. As soon as the doors closed, I let out a huge sigh.

"That was so close! I think I've had enough of winging it for one day. Let's go get a coffee."

It wasn't long before we'd found a table outside the snack bar, and with the bundle of cash I now had, I treated Amy to coffee and a plate of pastries. It was still early, and we had hours before Cassie would be back. I opened my bag to check the time on my phone... "I've still got the spare key! Damnit, I forgot to hand it in on the way out. I was just so relieved to have gotten away with it, I plain forgot. I'll have to go back," I groaned.

"Pah!" Amy spat, grabbing the key and dropping it into a nearby plant pot. "You heard the receptionist—lost keys are charged to the room. Let Cassie, the bitch deal with it. It's the least she can do."

"Ooh, you are wicked!"

We sat in comfortable silence for a few minutes, sipping coffee and watching the world go by. It had only been two days, but with everything we'd been through, it felt like Amy was an old friend.

"I really do appreciate everything you've done to help me, Amy," I said, breaking the silence.

"I know it's not been the best of circumstances, but in a way, it's been fun," she replied. Then quickly added, "But of course, I haven't had the worry of losing my boyfriend."

"I agree. I've enjoyed your company, and I certainly couldn't have come this far without you. And we've had some fun moments in between spying, breaking and entering, lying and impersonating someone," I said, making Amy burst out laughing. "I still can't believe we did all that!"

"I needed this break, but what should we do next? We've confirmed that Cassie is involved, and we know she is working at the castle. Do you think she's got him hidden up there?" Amy glanced up the hill to the castle.

"Before I left Scott, he said that the castle is closed at the moment. So, either she was lying about that too, or she's managed to blag her way into getting the key. Given what she said to you yesterday, it would be plausible for her to want to check out the place before the work started."

"So, do you fancy a trip up there? It's the only place I can imagine he'd be, and if he's not, we resort to plan A and confront her."

"Sounds like we have a plan and our new quest," I agreed.

As we discovered earlier, the bus route went up the hill and stopped very close to the castle. Up close, we could see that part of the castle was just ruins, odd piles of stone that suggested it had been a much bigger building. The main central part looked in good repair, though, with a huge wooden door in the centre, chained and padlocked to an iron ring. We wandered round until we reached a fenced off area with a sign in Spanish, but thankfully translated to English too—Staff only!

"I bet she's through there," Amy said, trying the latch on the gate. It opened. Beyond was a small courtyard filled with builders' sacks of stone and cement, and various tools. There didn't seem to be any sign of workmen, though. We followed the wall round to the back of the building until we found another door, and this one was open.

"You ready for this?" I checked.

"Well, we've come this far…" Amy peeped inside.

It led to what looked like a staffroom, with a small kitchen area at one end and seating at the other. Three other doors lead off it. Instinctively, I went to check the left-hand door first, but it was just a storeroom, with a couple of toilet stalls. Next, the middle door led out into the main area of the old castle. I guessed this was the bit the public could look around. Murals adorned the walls opposite a huge stone fireplace. Some were faded, and others were broken and chipped—lots of work for Scott to do when this nightmare was over. We had a quick glance round, but there was nowhere to lock up a person, as all the rooms were open.

"Back to try the third door, Hun?"

I nodded and followed Amy. Annoyingly, this one was locked, but maybe there was a reason for this. I banged on the door and shouted. "Scott! Hello! Scott, are you in there?"

I listened, my ear to the door. I could hear a faint voice—it sounded like Scott. Someone was locked in there, at least.

"Nooooo!"

Amy and I spun round as Cassie came charging in through the back door. She stopped in surprise when she saw Amy.

"You? What are you doing here? This place is closed to the public. You shouldn't be here."

"Give me the key, Cassie," I demanded. "Now!"

"Alana... what? How did you...?" Cassie faltered, then pulled herself together. "He doesn't want you anymore. He loves me. Go home, Alana, you're just making a fool of yourself."

"You've got him locked up in a frigging castle, you crazy bitch," Amy snarled.

Cassie took a step back. "He just needs some time to adjust to the situation, time away from you," she snapped back at me.

"Give me the key now, or I'm calling the police…" I started, but Amy lunged forwards and grabbed the bunch of keys from her hand. Panicked, Cassie turned and ran.

"You phone for the police while I get him out," I yelled, taking the keys off her.

I fumbled finding the right key, but finally, I opened the door to find another storeroom stacked with broken furniture and paintings.

"Scott?"

"Lana, thank goodness! I'm back here," the welcome sound of Scott's voice called from behind an old wooden bookcase.

I ran in, skirting around the piles of clutter, and finally found him. He sat on a camp bed, one wrist handcuffed to an iron ring in the stone wall. Tears welled up as I hugged him. The tension of the last few days, the fear, the relief and then the horror of finding him chained like this, all flooded out. Finally, I could speak.

"Are you okay? Are you hurt?" was all I could think of to say.

"No, I'm good now you're here. She's crazy, but at least she brought me food and water every day. Apart from a banging headache on the first day, I'm okay. How on earth did you find me?"

"I made a friend, Amy. She's calling the police right now. We need to get you out of here. Let me go see where Amy is and check if the key to these handcuffs is with the other ones."

After the last few days of stressful searching, I just needed a bit of luck. I prayed the key would be on the bunch Amy had taken from Cassie, and my prayers were answered. Scott was finally free. We wandered out, hand in hand, to find Amy.

Amy reappeared, frustrated. "I can't get a phone signal anywhere up here…oh my god, Scott!" She launched herself at Scott and hugged us both tightly.

Scott, a little bemused, grinned back. "I guess you must be Amy, then? I have you to thank, I hear."

"Well, we made a good team," she replied. "That crazy bitch went running off down the hill, but I checked the bus times when I was wandering round trying to get a phone signal and there's one due in about three minutes. You can tell us all on the bus ride home."

"I'd rather not discuss it in public," Scott replied. "Why don't we get back to the hotel? We can ring the police from there—I just want to get that over with. And then I will tell you how I ended up locked in this dammed castle!"

"Good idea," I agreed. "Plus, we have tales to tell about our daring rescue."

Back at the hotel, the receptionist phoned the police for us and ushered us into an office. We were interviewed separately, but Amy and I had agreed on the bus, to leave out the bit about searching Cassie's room. The police assured us they would deal with Cassie, and finally, we were free to go.

"Miss Meadows?"

I turned to see the kind receptionist from the first day, beckoning me over. Wearily, I approached the desk.

"Your new room key, deluxe double room, courtesy of the hotel. Just drop off the other key once you've had time to move your belongings over."

"I don't know about you two, but I desperately need a shower, and I'm starving!" Scott said. "How about we meet back at the restaurant in 20 minutes or so?"

"Seriously? You're going to keep me waiting another 20 minutes? Okay, but don't you dare tell the tale until I'm there." Amy warned with a grin.

Finally, we were all sat in the restaurant. As I'd expected, Scott loved the vast array of dishes on the buffet. He'd piled his plate high, but after the few days of living on sandwiches and water, I didn't blame him.

"I can't wait any longer," Amy said. "Go on, what on earth happened?"

In between mouthfuls, Scott told his side of the tale: "I handed Lana the case, then sat back in the taxi to pay the driver, and out of nowhere, Cassie appeared. I was shocked to see her here. Then, she got into the car, rattled off something in Spanish to the driver, and before I knew it, he was turning the car round and driving away. I yelled at Cassie to explain, and she said there was a big problem with the contract, and I was needed immediately. Of course, I argued that I couldn't just leave you without explaining, and demanded we turn back. The poor driver didn't know what to do and just kept driving.

I tried phoning you, but there was no signal. Cassie assured me I'd be able to ring you as soon as I got to the castle, and it was only a five minutes' drive away. We got there; she had keys and unlocked the door, saying the manager of the Spanish office was on his way. I tried to call many times, but as you discovered, Amy, there is no signal up there. It was so hot, and when Cassie gave me a glass of water, I welcomed it. I don't remember much after that until I woke, chained up, and with a killer headache. I can only assume she drugged me with something."

"That's unbelievable! Why would she do this?" Amy asked.

"And how did she know where you'd be? That's the bit I don't get," I added.

"When she first started working with us, she was great, really efficient—it was just before the Spanish contract was secured. She did all the admin work to organise the logistics, and being fluent in Spanish, she liaised with the Spanish office. Stupidly, I also discussed my plans to come here for a holiday to suss out the area, and as soon as you found this hotel deal, she found the flights for me to book. She's known every detail because I stupidly told her."

"But you couldn't have known how crazy she was. It's not your fault," I reassured him.

"That's not all, though. I didn't want to tell you the full story, because we were planning on moving here, and I knew she'd be gone from the company once I returned—it didn't seem worth the upset. Her initial friendly behaviour started to get a bit uncomfortable. She'd appear at my office with a document to sign or something, and then linger to talk, only leaving when I basically ordered her to go. I had to get quite brutal, but it didn't deter her. Then her overly friendly behaviour switched to outright flirting. She even suggested I should dump you and take her instead. I'd finally had enough and made a complaint to the boss. He promised to have a word with her, and her behaviour towards me improved slightly. I kept it from you because I didn't want to worry you, Lana. I knew you needed this holiday just as much as I did. Then, the week before we left, she went off sick, and I was so relieved. I put her out of my mind completely. Now I realise she'd already made plans to come here."

"What a conniving bitch!" Amy added.

"I guess if she knew our flight times, she only had to lurk around the hotel waiting for the right opportunity to make her move," I deduced.

"Yes, I think she truly believed we had a connection, and that as soon as I saw her out here, I'd change my plans to be with her. It's sad really, she's clearly not well. Or maybe I'm just too irresistible," Scott added, laughing. "Okay, I need to eat this colossal feast while you two tell me about your adventures."

Amy and I took it in turns to explain, with a few embellishments from Amy along the way. It was obvious now that the mystery caller who changed our room booking was Cassie—she must have been planning it for weeks. Finally, we finished the tale.

"So, what are your plans for the rest of the holiday?" Amy asked.

"Anything that doesn't involve going anywhere near that castle!" Scott joked. "I don't want to see the place again until the job starts, and I have control of the keys."

"I second that!" I agreed. "Now, who wants cocktails? I think we deserve them."

No Fairytale

A fairytale gown and a walk in the forest.

Once upon a time, there lived a beautiful princess. She met a handsome stranger from a far-off land, who just happened to be a prince. They soon married and lived happily ever after in peace and harmony….

Wouldn't that be lovely? Sadly, not all fairytales are so idyllic, and despite my attire, this is definitely no fairytale. So, here I am, deep in the forest, trying to stop this ridiculous gown from snagging on brambles as I hastily make my way to the clearing. From there, it's thankfully only a few minutes' walk to the small access road where I left my car earlier this morning. I'm nearly there—thank goodness I had the foresight to wear trainers under this voluminous skirt.

*****

We came at dawn to capture that special light as the first sunbeams filter through the trees, appearing to radiate from a single distant source. *Komorebi*, I believe the Japanese call it; they have such beautiful words to encompass the entire mood and feeling of what we only describe. My photographer husband delighted at the way the light danced across the scarlet fabric of my fairytale gown, following blindly as I wandered farther, in search of the perfect setting. I was reluctant at first, when Nick suggested I model for him—he wanted to create an advertising campaign to entice new customers to book a photoshoot. Dressing up for a walk in my favourite place did seem like fun, if a little less practical than my usual jeans and t-shirt. I soon lost my inhibitions as I breathed in the glorious earthy scents, and Nick snapped away, oblivious to anything beyond the viewfinder.

The familiar landmarks we passed, the thicket of spiky holly with a secret hollow inside, the ancient oak with boughs that reached down to provide an easy foothold, the bank of delicate indigo belladonna beneath towering foxgloves, brought memories of long summers and magical adventures, while Mum foraged for blackberries and wild mushrooms. The knowledge engrained and the delight of free food had carried forward into adulthood, and I still tramped familiar paths with my basket of berries. I had hoped Nick would share my passion, but no, he was a big-city boy through and through. This photoshoot was one of the rare times I'd been able to coax him away from a concrete path and he seemed more alive than ever. I hoped the experience would inspire him to join me on future walks, and I chattered about how we could do this every weekend. Nick shushed me, more engaged with the camera than the conversation.

Nick urged that we only stop for a quick break, as he needed to get back soon for a work meeting. I carefully draped my skirts over a fallen log that conveniently served as a seat and poured us both coffee from the thermos Nick insisted on bringing. I savoured the moment, soaking up the glorious sunshine. Nick stood, sipped his coffee and fiddled with his camera settings. Inevitably, the coffee sent Nick off searching for a 'private' place to attend to a call of nature, but not before instructing me to guard his equipment. Seriously? Who did he think was going to be hiding behind a tree, waiting to steal a camera at this time of the morning? I chuckled at Nick's city ways and picked up his mobile to check the time—with no pockets, I'd left mine in the car. A flurry of notifications pinged in as the screen lit up…

*****

The sunbeams disappeared as grey clouds drifted overhead. I managed to reach the car as the first raindrops splashed through the leaves. They mixed with the tears soaking my cheeks. I hadn't thought rationally earlier. I just gathered up my skirts and ran, weaving between the trees, needing to get as far away from my cheating husband as possible. I sat watching the rivers of rain streaming down the car windscreen, distorting the scene beyond—I imagined Nick too intent on keeping his precious camera dry to notice my absence. Then I imagined him slowly realising he was alone, deep in unfamiliar territory. I pictured his panic when he realised his guide back to civilisation had disappeared. I assumed that right about now, he was searching for the phone that sat on the passenger seat next to me.

I shrugged off any guilt at leaving him stranded as I read back through the messages. They started with flirtatious jokes that soon developed into plans for covert meetings. A quick checking of dates showed their trysts coincided with my weekly woodland wanders, the walks that Nick avoided because he was 'too busy with work'. I remembered the many times he'd seemed distant when I'd rambled on about all my foraging finds, while rinsing bowls of plump black berries—I'd just assumed him weary from work. It was the final text that snapped me out of my misery—*Sorry I couldn't do the shoot this morning. Want to meet up after you drop her home?*

My tummy rumbled. Despite the surge of emotions churning, I was hungry. Nick would be getting hungry, too. Would he pick berries to stave off hunger pangs as he wandered, wet and lost? The belladonna berries were ripening very close to where I'd abandoned him. Would Nick remember me chattering away about wildflowers? Would he remember their other name—deadly nightshade—or that ingesting them would cause hallucinations, convulsions and eventually death? I shrugged; it was no longer my problem.

The rain eased off; it was time for this princess to drive home, alone. But first, I needed to send a message to my now ex-best friend to come rescue *her* prince from the forest—that is, if she could find him. I switched off Nick's phone, wiped my eyes and set off, spurred on by the thought of breakfast, a hot coffee and getting changed out of this silly dress. This fairytale was over, and it was time to create a new love story.

The Ring

People watching and a strange encounter.

"Are you sure this is the right day, Rosie?" Phil asked, as he unpacked the flask from the backpack.

I shared out the last of the coffee and handed Phil a cup. "Yes, you know it is. I've had it marked in the diary all year."

"I don't think he's coming. If he's not here by the time we've finished our coffee, we'll go. We've been here three hours already, and it really was a long shot that he'd turn up."

"Let's just stay another hour. Please?" I pleaded. I stuck my hand in my pocket, feeling for the ring. It was still there.

Last year...

"Race you to the top!"

As per usual, Phil cheated and set off running before he finished the sentence. I jogged the last few steps, letting him win. "Look at that view! It's glorious up here today. It's worth the trek up here just for that view."

"Yes, and it's the perfect place for a picnic. I'm starving!" Phil replied, unpacking his backpack. "Are you going to come join me? Rosie? Hello…earth to Rosie. Are you people-watching again?"

"Yeah, sorry. Do you see that couple over there? The young man and that old lady?"

"Yes, what about them? Rosie, can you be a bit more subtle? You're staring."

"Oops! I just wonder what their story is. He looks sad and her clothing seems oddly inappropriate for a trek up a hill. What's he doing?" I watched as he picked up a rock and added it to a small pile.

"Nosy Rosie strikes again! Leave them in peace and come have something to eat. I'm…"

"Starving? Yeah, you're always hungry," I giggled as I unwrapped the sandwiches. I couldn't help glancing over at the odd couple as we ate our lunch. "He's leaving."

"So?" Phil rolled his eyes. "We came up here to see the view, not stare at random strangers."

"Yes, but look! He's gone back down the rocky path and left the old lady on her own. Do you think she's OK?"

Phil glanced over. "She looks fine to me. Maybe she is going to take the easy path down, or maybe they weren't even here together."

"I'm going to talk to her. Check she's OK."

"Seriously, Rosie?"

I heard Phil muttering something, but my mind was made up. I wandered over to where the lady was sitting on a large boulder. Up close, I could see that the man had been adding rocks to a small cairn. I sat close to the lady and smiled, but she seemed lost in thought.

"It's so beautiful up here, isn't it?" I said.

"Yes, it was one of our favourite places when we were young. Now, we just come here once a year," she replied, still gazing at the path the man had taken.

"We love it here too. That's my husband over there," I said, pointing.

"He looks nice. My son's getting married next year."

"Was that your son who was here earlier?"

"Yes, that was James. We used to bring him here when he was little. He moved to Canada a few years ago to be close to his fiancé's family, but he comes back to visit me. We make the trip up here on the same day every year."

My curiosity was burning, but before I could ask more, she continued.

"This will be my last trip up here and I'm so annoyed at myself. Look!" The old lady handed me a gold wedding ring inset with four tiny diamonds. "I forgot to give him this, and now he's gone, and I won't be able to get it to him."

I looked at the ring. There were two names engraved inside: James and Emily. I went to hand back the ring, but she closed my hand over it.

"Will you give it to him for me, please?"

"Well, I'm not sure, I don't know him…" I faltered, not quite knowing what to say.

"It would make me happy. I won't make it to the wedding, but if you give him this ring, I can be a part of it in a small way." The old lady gazed into the distance again while I pondered what to do. *We do this walk often; it would be no hardship to come back.* "So, he'll be back here next year?"

"Yes, dear. Same day, every year."

I said my goodbyes, promised I would do my best to get the ring to her son, then wandered back over to Phil.

"So, did you satisfy your nosiness, then?" Phil asked.

I filled him in on the strange conversation we'd had and showed him the ring.

"She sounds a bit loopy to me. Why didn't she just post it to her son? Surely that's easier than trusting a random, nosy stranger to return in a year. Don't you think that's a bit odd?" Phil shook his head.

"Well, when you say it like that, yes, it does sound odd. Maybe I should give it back to her and suggest she posts it instead." I glanced back towards the rock cairn. "Too late, she's gone. And I did make her a promise…"

Present day...

"Look Phil, there's a man coming up the path. Do you think that could be him?"

"I don't know. Don't go rushing over, Rosie. Let's just wait until he gets closer."

The man headed straight to the cairn and tidied the fallen rocks back into place. "You stay here. I'll go ask him if his name is James." I ignored Phil's exasperated sigh and wandered over.

"Hi, I know this is going to sound weird, but is your name James?"

The man nodded and stared in confusion. It was the look of someone trying to work out whether he knew me.

"You were here last year, so were we. I spoke to your mum after you left and..."

"I was here, but you have the wrong person," he replied abruptly.

I held out the ring for him to see. "Oh, I'm sorry, I was supposed to give this ring to a James who comes here on the same day every year." I cringed inwardly as I turned to leave.

"Wait, I don't understand, but that looks like my mum's ring. Let me have a closer look."

"The lady I spoke to wanted her James to have it for his wedding. She had the names James and Emily engraved inside," I added.

"Emily's my fiancé. We're getting married in a couple of months," he replied, looking even more confused as he examined the ring.

"So, I have got the right James then?"

James faltered. "I… I think so, but I just don't get it. It's true I come here every year, but last year was the first time I came alone. I came to scatter Mum's ashes with my dad's."

The Christmas Box

Sibling rivalries kill the festive cheer.

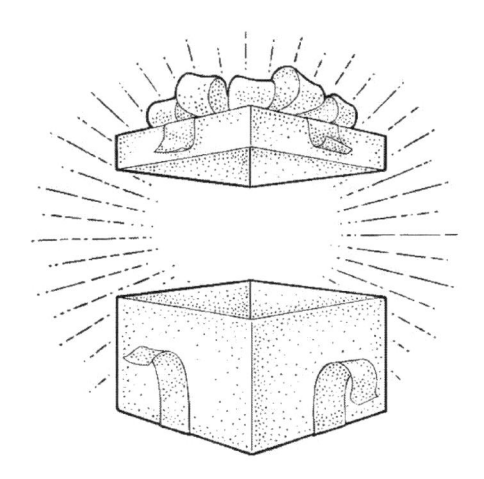

I am not looking forward to Christmas this year!

I can't remember when we started to grow apart. Maybe it was when Lucy went to university to study law, or perhaps when Kat got her swanky PR job in London. Liz and I were always the quiet ones, and I guess out of my three sisters, she's the one I tolerate most, but only just. Spending the weekend with just Liz might be manageable, but all four of us together, with Mum and Gran, in Gran's little cottage….

We've only been here for an hour and already, Kat's taken the limelight, bragging about celebs she's met. Liz is doing a good job of ignoring her, her head in a book. Gran's nodding, pretending to be impressed, but I can tell she hasn't a clue who Kat is waffling on about. Mum is doing the 'behave yourself' glare, but I'm too busy focusing on Lucy to care. It's actually quite comical watching Lucy's eye-rolling disdain—I can just imagine the snarky comments going through her mind, and the amount of restraint it's taking to stay polite in front of Gran.

Mum gave us all the pep talk before we arrived at Gran's. "Be nice, please. I just want one last Christmas with us all together…" We'd all promised, but there's only so long before sibling rivalries and past arguments rise to the surface. For Mum's and Gran's sake, I'm trying not to tell Kat to shut up and let someone else speak for a change.

Gran waited for Kat to take a breath and stood up. "I need you girls to do me a favour…"

"Oh, of course, Gran, what do you want?" Lucy piped up, using her annoying big sister voice.

"I need you to get my Christmas box out of the attic. It's big though. It'll need all four of you to carry it."

Kat glanced at her fancy trouser suit, clearly not impressed by the prospect of clambering around in a dusty attic. "OK, Gran. But you go first, Cass. I'm not going up there if there are spiders."

"Why me?" I snapped back, but caught Mum's eye, pleading with me to be nice. "OK then, follow me. Let's get Gran's box."

"What's in it, Gran?" Liz asked.

"You'll see when you get up there." Gran giggled.

I peeped my head through the hatch and flicked the light switch. "No spiders, just a bit of dust—you'll be okay Kat." I was secretly hoping a big fat spider would drop down on her head, but the attic was reasonably clear, just two piles of boxes at the far side. I climbed in to give the others room to follow.

"Right, which one's the Christmas box? You two look on that side, Kat, you help me over here," Lucy demanded.

Liz and I shared a look. We were so used to her bossiness, but it was easier to just ignore her. We shuffled over to the far side and started to lift boxes down so we could see the labels, penned in Gran's cursive scrawl.

SLAM!

"What the hell was that?" Kat squealed.

"The hatch just fell down," I said, stating the obvious. "No big deal."

Liz crawled over to lift it up again. "It won't budge. It's stuck!"

"Don't be silly," Lucy said, pushing her out of the way and pulling on the ring to lift it. It was stuck fast. "Why didn't you prop it up, Kat? You were the last up here."

"Don't blame me. I didn't want to come up here in the first place. MUM! GRAN! We're stuck! HELP!" Kat shouted until it was obvious nobody was coming to get us out.

"Mum was going to pop to the shop, and I bet Gran's not got her hearing aids tuned in," I reasoned. "Let's find the box and when Mum gets back, I'm sure she'll come to look for us."

Kat grumbled, Lucy begrudgingly agreed that was the best plan, and Liz had already started shuffling boxes around.

"I've found it!" Liz said. We all crowded round to see what was in it. It wasn't even that big, certainly not big enough to need four of us to carry it. Lucy opened the lid. We glanced at each other in confusion, expecting Christmassy stuff, but instead, there was a broken ballerina figurine, held together with yellowing sticky tape.

"What the hell?" Kat moaned, picking it up.

"Wait, I remember this. It's the ballerina Mum gave to Gran," Liz said. "I must have been around 10 years old. I was in the kitchen and Clover came bounding in and knocked it off the dresser—the head fell off. You were supposed to be watching the dog, Cass, and I didn't want you to get in trouble, so I carefully put it back, balancing the head on top."

"Seriously?" Kat laughed. "All these years and I thought you'd broken it, Liz. The head rolled off as you came out of the kitchen. I quickly kicked it under the table before Gran saw it."

"And then Lucy sat at the table swinging her feet. She kicked it towards me. I thought Lucy had broken it, so I stuck it together with sticky tape and put it back on the dresser," I added. "I didn't want her to get in trouble either."

Lucy giggled. "That was a fun Christmas, wasn't it? We had each other's backs when we were little."

"Yeah," I added. "It was us against the world. Do you remember our secret sisters' club?"

"Hey, there's something else in the box," Liz said, pulling out a piece of paper. We crowded round to read Gran's spidery handwriting:

'I hope this box has helped you find your Christmas cheer. The password to open the hatch is your old catchphrase.

Love Gran

P.S. I never did like that ballerina, but don't tell your mum. Our secret!'

We all linked our little fingers together and shouted in unison: "Sisters Forever!"

The hatch opened.

Red Lights

The trip of a lifetime.

The hypnotic shush of the waves shifting the shingle lulls me into a peaceful trance. Eyes closed; I can still see the red imprint of a glowing sun in a cloudless sky burning through my eyelids. A momentary flicker of guilt passes over. I should go for a walk, paddle in the surf, or read, but I sit motionless until the feelings drift away. The book I couldn't wait to start sits beside me full of promises of adventure and escape, but the bookmark hasn't moved from inside the cover. It's just too hot to do much other than sit; sit and ponder.

I shuffle further under the shade, but the thin fabric gives little protection from the scorching heat. A gentle sea breeze brings a little reprieve, but it is short-lived.

A flurry of giggles and excited chatter pulls me from my musings. I watch as children run, shedding clothes on the sand, as they race to paddle in the sea. A mum follows close behind, brandishing a bottle of sun cream, but it's too late, the children are already splashing through the foamy waves. She sighs and smiles, instead collecting their discarded t-shirts and shorts. Oh, to have that much energy.

The breeze lifts my hair, cooling the rivulets of sweat running down the back of my neck. And with it, scents of tropical fruit, pineapple, and mango drift by. I breathe them in, and they mingle with the fresh, salty air. Down the beach, a waiter pulls a wagon full of sodas. I wave him over. An ice-cold cola is just what I need. Maybe it will give me the motivation to read or go paddle in the sea. I envy the children lying in the cool water.

The waiter sees me and ambles over as I fumble in my purse for some change. Savouring the moment, I first hold the can to my forehead, then down to my chest. The condensation soaks my flimsy sundress, but it's cooling at least. I sip at first, then gulp down the rest, feeling the motivation to move flood back with every mouthful.

A gust of wind catches my sunhat, and the intense scarlet light fades to gold. I take a last look round this tranquil paradise. The monotonous roar of the surf intensifies to a rattly growl, a flash of green, and I feel myself lurch forwards, and back...

***

Sadly, I watch the sea and sand blur into the distance until I can no longer see the billboard through the window. I shift uncomfortably as the broken heater blasts tepid air into an already warm car. A heady aroma of sweet mango from the air freshener blends with the stench of sweat and exhaust fumes, and I long for the sea breeze of moments ago to refresh my senses, but it's long gone.

Up ahead, the traffic lights switched to amber. I gazed out of the passenger window, trying to see what new billboards have been pasted up since I last travelled this route. I quickly take in the adverts and wonder which I will land on: a smiling family enjoying the new meal deal at McDonalds, Shady Oaks Retirement Home welcoming an old couple, a futuristic ship hovering over WC137064 alien planet in some new sci-fi film, and Happy Pets Veterinary Clinic offering a 10% discount to new customers. Anything would be better than this intense heat.

Thank goodness! The light changes to red. The car rolls to a stop and I close my eyes once more, waiting to be transported to the world within the glossy billboard image.

***

The idling engine switches to a metallic whirring, an alarm sounds, bright lights flash and my eyes spring open. Instinctively, I reach forward and tap the screen to silence the noise. I take a moment to enjoy the refreshing cool air, blasting through shiny steel vents above me, then I gaze in wonder at the vast expanse of space through the viewport of my ship. I glance over at my co-pilot and match her grin. Her blue skin and black, almond-shaped eyes would have seemed so incongruous within my last billboard trip, but she seems perfectly natural in this futuristic setting.

She hits a few buttons on the panel above; I hear the engine noise shift, deepening in tone, and I know instinctively that we're slowing down. A large planet slowly comes into view; we're preparing to land. My giant ship gradually becomes dwarfed as we approach the surface. My fingers tap keys, while my co-pilot navigates between towering metal structures. Then we descend to land on a dazzling, metallic blue roof that shimmers under the glare of twin suns.

I do love these billboard escapes, and this one is going to be an adventure…

Scarlett And The Wolf

A modern-day fairytale.

"Here Scarlett, drop this bag round at your gran's place on your way to the club, will you?"

Scarlett grimaced at her mum and glanced in the bag: a packet of custard creams and the latest copy of OK magazine.

"Your gran asked me to pick them up for her, but I haven't had a chance to go see her today."

Scarlett sighed, and pulled her red hoodie up over her tangled brown curls. "Okay, Mum," she yelled as she slipped out the door.

"Oh, and Scarlett… don't cut through the Forest Estate, it's not safe at this time of night."

"Don't worry, Mum, I won't," she yelled over her shoulder.

"And stay away from that Wolf boy. He's bad news, that one."

Scarlett sighed and carried on. She had no intention of going the long way round to Gran's nursing home. She glanced back to check Mum wasn't watching and nipped down the ginnel to the Forest Estate.

"Alright Red?" a figure slunk out of the shadows, startling her. Scarlett's heart was still pounding when she recognised the sly grin of Jackson Wolf. He wasn't quite as bad as Mum made him out to be, but he did have a habit of appearing in all the wrong places.

"Shit, Jackson! Don't do that. You know I'm not supposed to hang out with you. If Mum sees…"

"What ya got there, Red? Anything for me?"

"Nah, just some stuff for my gran. I'll drop this off and see you at the club later. Now go before my mum catches us chatting."

Jackson started to protest, but paused as Scarlett shushed him, and pulled out her buzzing phone. She glared at Jackson to keep him quiet while she answered the call.

"Hi Gran… Yes, I'm on my way now. I'll be there in ten… Tell you what, I'll bang on your window so you can buzz me in, save you getting out of bed. See ya soon… Love you too."

"Love you too Granny darling," mimicked Jackson.

"Sod off, Wolf! I'll catch you later."

Jackson Wolf leapt on his bike and blew her a kiss as he cycled away. Scarlett giggled as she watched him disappear into the Forest Estate. He wasn't that bad, a cocky sod maybe, but his bad reputation was mainly down to the hype he'd spread himself. It was all about image on the Forest.

Ten minutes later, Scarlett arrived at the Shadewood Nursing Home. As planned, she tapped on Gran's window and ran around to the door before the buzzer stopped. Five minutes with Gran, then she'd be off to the club. The curtains were drawn, and by the bundle of covers, it looked like Gran was tucked up in bed. She must have been barely awake when she pressed the door buzzer, to have fallen asleep again so quickly. Still, it worked in her favour.

Scarlett tiptoed to the bed. If she could quietly leave the bag without waking her gran, she could get away without a lecture about the evils of drink, drugs, and bad boys—Gran meant well, but she did go on a bit.

Suddenly, there was a flush of water, and the bathroom door flung open, flooding the room with light. Scarlett froze, her eyes flicking between the bedcovers and Gran. The covers were shaking.

"Oh, hello love! Did your mother send you over with my biccies?" said Gran as she flicked back the patchwork quilt to climb in.

"Mmm, biccies!" growled a voice from under the covers.

Scarlett squealed as she recognised the voice, but Gran screamed, as Jackson leapt from the bed, roaring with laughter.

"Help! Security!" Gran screamed, brandishing her walking stick. "Thief!"

Jackson ducked under the waving stick, barged past Scarlett, and legged it out of the door. "Laters, Red!" he called and winked over his shoulder.

Scarlett stifled a laugh, as Jackson dodged old Bailey's zimmer frame, and ducked out of the clutches of the matronly receptionist. With a wave and a cheeky grin, he sped off, chased by three staff members and a stick-wielding granny.

Scarlett looked around. The foyer was empty and, in their haste to catch Wolf, they'd left the door to the medical room open. Perfect! She hastily grabbed as many tubs of pills as she could stash in her backpack. Casually, she sauntered outside to where Gran was still shouting obscenities at Jackson as he disappeared into the Forest Estate.

"You alright, Gran?" Scarlett asked. "I'll sort Jackson Wolf out for you. Don't you worry."

"That Wolf boy better not have stolen my custard creams! If I catch him…" Granny hobbled back to the room, muttering threats under her breath.

"It's okay, Gran. Your biccies are safe. Let's get you back into bed."

Scarlett realised Jackson must have snuck ahead, getting Gran to buzz him in, thinking it was her granddaughter. The sneaky sod! She'd definitely have words with him later! Still, his stupid prank had worked in her favour. Kissing Gran goodbye, she left slowly, careful to keep her backpack from rattling as she passed the front desk.

The Forest Youth Club was buzzing by the time Scarlett got there. The doorman gave her a wink and ushered her in; she was a regular and knew all the staff. Her ready smile and polite manners had gotten her a reputation for being a 'lovely young lady'. Ha, if only they knew!

Security cameras covered most of the club, but there was a blind spot in the corner booth. Scarlett's gang always made sure they grabbed that table for their base. Not that anyone would suspect her of anything dodgy, but better to be careful. A couple of the guys were already there, so she nipped to the loo to check out her haul from the nursing home. She sorted through the containers, some she'd have to chuck away, but she got plenty of good stuff too. It'd bring in a tidy sum from the local druggies.

"What ya got there, Red?"

"Bloody hell, Wolf! You scared the shit outa me. What ya doing lurking in the ladies' loos?" For the second time today, Scarlett's heart was pounding thanks to Jackson Wolf. How did he always manage to sneak up on her like that? "I can't believe you pulled that prank on Gran. You're bad, Wolf!"

Jackson stuck his hand in Scarlett's backpack and pulled out a tub of pills. He rattled them in her face, shaking his head and tutting.

"I may be a bad Wolf, but you're the big bad Red in the hood."

The Witch in the Woods

Deception for protection.

"Leave here now!" she snarled, pointing her crooked staff at the boys sneaking down the overgrown path.

"The witch!" the biggest boy yelled. "Quick, leg it!"

Squealing, the three boys turned and ran, thorny brambles tearing at bare legs as they bolted. The littlest one stumbled over a fallen branch, face-planted in the leaf mulch, and squealed in fear.

"Help, she's gonna get me!"

His older brother glanced back, searched the trees for movement behind them, then quickly hoicked him back to his feet by the hood of his jacket. Still grasping the hood, he half dragged the boy, guiding him through the trees to safety.

Ducking under branches and weaving through the thick undergrowth, they ran, until finally, they reached the main road and collapsed, panting on the pavement.

"Do you think she cursed us, Charlie?"

"Nah, I think we got away in time. What's the evil witch doing in those woods, anyway? You okay, Kyle, Shaun?" Charlie plonked himself down next to his youngest brother.

"Dunno, but I'm never going back—ever!" Kyle cried, rubbing at the itchy white bumps forming on his bare legs. "Think I ran through every single nettle. That place is definitely cursed."

"It don't scare me," Shaun mocked, brandishing a stick towards the dark woods.

"Yeah right!" Charlie laughed. "You weren't so brave when you saw the witch, were you? You set off running before she even spoke."

"Yeah Shaun," Kyle mocked, "dare you to go back on your own, at night."

"Okay, so she made me jump just appearing out of nowhere, but I only ran because it's nearly teatime and Mum will shout if we're late."

"Now that is scary," Charlie chuckled. "Come on, and do not tell her we went into those woods."

*****

The witch grinned as she continued down the path. Gnarly roots reached out of the tangled undergrowth, threatened to trip unsuspecting trespassers. She wondered how many scratches the boys had endured on their flight of terror. It was unlikely they'd be back.

The shady trees soon opened into a sunny glade. She paused; this view always took her breath away. Dragonflies flitted over the pond, competing for a tasty snack with the frogs lazing amidst the lilies. Movement on the far bank caught her attention—the female water vole was nibbling on the reeds, while her pups peeped from the burrow. Here, the woodland silence was replaced by the whir of wings and joyful birdsong.

She added more seeds to her bird table, then settled herself down on the bank and took out a book from the pocket of her woollen cloak. It was the perfect place for a peaceful read. She sighed contentedly and opened the book.

When she moved here ten years ago, the pond was just a stagnant pool filled with litter from the local youths. Posting 'Private Land' and 'Keep Out!' signs hadn't deterred the young hooligans either. Her clean-up efforts seemed in vain, as every day, new crisp packets floated on the water's surface, and squashed cans and sweet wrappers littered the bank. She carried on, undeterred. This small patch of private woodland that bordered her garden was the main reason she'd chosen to buy the cottage, and she was determined to restore it to a place of beauty.

The first time she'd scared the kids away had been accidental. She'd stood watching them from the shadows, contemplating what reception she'd get if she challenged the youths to take their litter home. A chilly breeze whistled through the branches, prompting her to pull her cloak around her. Then using a stick to steady herself, she stepped out of the trees to speak to them. Suddenly, one of the lads spotted her and jumped up, spooked, yelling, 'witch!'. His mates laughed, then their faces changed as they followed his gaze. She was about to call out to reassure them, but they were gone, hurtling through the trees after their mate.

She felt bad for scaring them, but later, when she examined her appearance in the full-length mirror, she saw why. Leaves and twigs were caught in her long, dark hair, giving her a wild and unkempt look. Add to that the forest green cloak—ideal for walking in the woods—and her favourite knobbly old walking stick. She had to admit, she did look like a scary witch from a storybook. The seeds of an idea started to form….

The following day, she took down the signs – they were useless anyway – and set about clearing the last lot of rubbish from the pond. She hung twisted homemade willow stars from the branches around the clearing, decorated with feathers and other woodland treasures she'd found on her walks. Next, she built a bird table out of branches, sprinkled seeds on top, and added a large candle in the middle to maintain the witchy illusion. Hand-painted pebbles formed a star around the base—perfect to attract wildlife and deter impressionable young litterers.

The scene was set, and it only took a few well-timed spooky appearances from the dark trees for rumours of the scary witch to spread. Imaginations ran wild, as children exaggerated their encounters—her walking stick became a magic staff, her foraging bag was full of poisonous plants, and the overgrown woods were clearly cursed. She laughed as she overheard the tales when she popped into town to do her shopping, but her plan was working. As the kids stopped using the pond as their hangout, so did the litter, and slowly the wildlife returned. She didn't mind keeping up the pretence if it meant a safe haven for the many endangered species that now thrived in her secret woodland oasis. They were here to stay and so, too, was the legend of the witch in the woods.

Secret Santa

Not all gifts are full of Christmas cheer.

It's the last day before the office closes for the Christmas holidays, and I'm counting down the minutes until I can take a well-earned break. I've already taken down the tinsel from around my desk to ensure a quick getaway; there's just one last thing to endure—the annual farce of Secret Santa, organised by our office gossip and self-appointed head of social events, Steph! I thought back to last year's Secret Santa and smirked...

Last year

Steph insisted on taking charge, bossing everyone around, and demanding we make more of an effort to get into the festive spirit. I rolled my eyes at Cindy, our secretary, and my best buddy in the office, and stuck a bit of holly on my monitor. Cindy chuckled and added a shiny red bow to the phone handset. Our attempts to annoy Steph backfired though as we both arrived the next morning to find our desks festooned in gaudy tinsel, and Santa hats hanging from our chairs, complete with post-it notes instructing us to wear them. Of course, Steph was already wearing hers, a sequined monstrosity with a giant fluffy pom pom, that bounced each time she flounced down into the office.

Then it was Secret Santa time, Steph made a big fuss over getting us each to write our names on a bit of paper—"fold it three times, Louise, come on, do it properly!"—then put it in the hat. She shook the hat dramatically, and drew out a name for herself, then went round while we each drew out a name.

"Now you must keep this secret. No cheating, Cindy. And remember, this is just for fun, the budget is £3," Steph explained, even though we all knew exactly how Secret Santa worked, not to mention the fact that she'd already sent round an email earlier that day, with tediously detailed instructions.

On the last day, we were summoned to receive our Secret Santa presents. Steph had been waiting at the door as we arrived that morning. She gathered in the labelled parcels and placed them in a giant sack. Now she was revelling in being the centre of attention, handing them out to each person in turn. My colleagues unwrapped bottles of bubble bath, selection boxes and candles, until there was just me and Steph left. She felt around in the sack and drew out a beautifully wrapped parcel.

"Oooh! This one's for me. How lovely!" she gushed as she tore off the paper. "Oh wow! These are my favourite chocolates, what a fabulous present. How did you guess what I wanted?"

I restrained myself from rolling my eyes at Cindy. It was common knowledge Steph had a stash of posh chocs in her top drawer. They would have been an easy choice for a present, but for the price—they were at least triple the budget she'd set. I glanced at the sack, just my present left, then we could all escape.

"Well, thank you, everyone. That's it, Happy Christmas!" Steph said, folding up the sack.

"Hey, what about Louise? She hasn't had her present yet, Steph," Cindy queried on my behalf.

"Oh, what a shame, Louise," Steph said, using her whiny baby voice. "You must have forgotten to put your name in the hat. Well, have a good holiday everyone and see you next year."

Cindy and I waited until she'd left…

"What a scam!" Cindy spat out. "I bet she bought those chocolates for herself to guarantee getting the best present."

"I wouldn't be surprised. She probably didn't put her own name in the hat…but if everyone else got a present, that would mean she was the one to draw out my name. I definitely put my name in there, and I saw her take a name out."

"What a cow! Here, you can share my bath bombs," Cindy said, ripping open the shiny box and handing over two. "Come on, let's get out of here."

Present Day

The events of the day were almost a carbon copy of last year—almost!

Steph was on top form, pom pom bobbing as she ceremoniously presented the sack of Secret Santa presents. Colleagues unwrapped the same array of cheap toiletries and festive gifts, making the relevant 'Ooh!' and 'How lovely!' remarks. I glanced round to see if I could work out who'd sent each gift. I suppressed the urge to grin as each person tried to mask their surprise that the gift they'd bought was being opened by someone other than the person they'd bought it for. As per Steph's secrecy rules, though, nobody dared to voice the mistake.

It was my turn next; I unwrapped a smelly candle. I was sure this was Cindy's contribution, judging by the confused look on her face.

"Okay, here's the last one. This must be mine," Steph said with glee, pulling out a similar sized parcel to last year's extravagant present.

"Hang on, Steph, that one's got Cindy's name on it," our manager, Carol, said, handing it over to Cindy.

"Wait! That can't be right..." Steph faltered and stopped. She watched in dismay as Cindy opened the large box of Steph's favourite chocolates.

"Ooh look Steph. One present must have fallen out of the sack," I exclaimed, smiling sweetly as I retrieved a small, badly wrapped present from under her desk. And it's got your name on it."

Steph unwrapped the package, muttered a begrudging, "thanks" and shoved the Poundshop socks in her handbag.

As Steph flounced out of the office, Cindy shot me a knowing look.

"You switched all the labels, didn't you?" she whispered.

I glanced over at Cindy and mouthed one word—"revenge!"

The Pitch

A perfect plan goes awry.

"So, you know the plan?"

"Yes, yes, we've been over it at least five times already, Beth. Trust me!" Dan reassured his nervous wife.

"I know, but I just want to talk it through one last time. It has to be perfect to secure the development grant. You know how much this means to me. This is five years of research and hard work, and it all hangs on their decision today."

"Okay, but I do know what I'm doing. I have the notes on my laptop, but I know them off by heart now."

"So, you go before the board, at 1.30pm, you do the presentation, run through the different phases of the prototype…" Beth started.

"Then dazzle them with the science," Dan cut her off. "Then at exactly 2pm, you appear for the demonstration. See, I got it. Trust me."

"Are you sure you have the coordinates of the place programmed in correctly?" Beth fussed.

"Yes, we've gone through it many times. I double-checked them after I went fishing yesterday, as you know. Look, you're just nervous, but it will be fine."

"I guess you're right. I'm just so excited to see how this goes. Now, you better get going. Good luck and I'll see you at 2."

Beth watched as Dan put his laptop and the device in the car, then gave him a final hug.

She had just enough time to check her outfit and makeup; she wanted her appearance to make a huge impact on the board. She'd chosen a long-sleeved black dress, figure hugging but not too tight, with a skirt that fell to just above her knees. She'd tried several, but both she and Dan agreed that this one was the perfect balance to stand out amongst the grey suits of her competition, yet still show her as a serious businesswoman.

1.26pm. Dan would be setting up the device and logging into the laptop in readiness. She toyed with the idea of sending a good luck text but she didn't want to distract him from the task.

Killing time, she ran a brush through her long hair and checked her makeup—it was perfect. The waiting was killing her. For the millionth time, she checked her device—it was charged, and the coordinates box, paired with the one on Dan's device, filled the screen. In the corner, the timer was set to 10 seconds, just waiting to be activated.

1.43 p.m. Dan would be onto the science bit now. They'd deliberately scripted it to sound technical, while keeping it vague enough to not divulge crucial details until the funding was secured. Dan had joked that it read like a Star Trek episode and rehearsed the pitch in his best Dr Spock voice. She'd laughed, but she knew that when she appeared for the demo, the wow factor would outweigh any confusion over Dan's explanation. His speech was merely to build suspense until its capabilities were revealed.

The last fifteen minutes seemed to drag on for hours, but she couldn't take her eyes off the clock. 1.29 p.m. Beth took a deep breath, picked up the device, and stood in the middle of the living room. Her arms ached as she mentally counted down the seconds; this prototype was quite large, built into the case of an old laptop, but with the funding, she'd be able to modify the design to be the size of a regular mobile phone.

Finally, the timer clicked and the ten second countdown started. Beth took another deep breath and prepared herself.

*****

Dan tried to read the room as he went through the pitch he'd rehearsed so many times. The board was made up of four women and three men. Their faces didn't give much away, attentive and curious, but whether he was convincing them, he didn't know. Still, it didn't matter. Beth would be the one to seal the deal.

It was time. Dan turned on the big screen behind him, which projected an image of his device screen, then he hit the button to start the timer.

Ten

Nine

Eight

Seven

Six…

*****

Beth counted down.

Five

Four

Three

Two…

The familiar scene of her living room faded as she was enveloped in a bubble of white light. Her earlier worries dissipated instantly. Despite many trial runs, this serene sensation still took her by surprise. It wasn't unpleasant, but it was a strange feeling, nonetheless. Outside her bubble, she watched a vibrant kaleidoscope of colours whizz by so quickly she couldn't grasp their form, just the perception of great speed from the stillness of the bubble. It felt like an eternity, but she knew from the trials it was only one second.

She smiled, ready to dazzle the board, but as the bubble dissipated, an icy splash of water hit her legs and she slipped back, landing on a large rock. Shock was quickly replaced with panic as she lifted the device out of the flowing water. 'Damn it, Dan! How the hell did you manage to program me to land in a river?' she cursed.

She scrambled to the bank and frantically assessed the damage. The device was thankfully still working, its screen open to receive new coordinates. Her appearance was not so fortunate though. Quickly, she poured the water from her shoes, squeezed the worst of it from her damp dress and finger combed her tousled hair. No time to worry, she sent a hurried text to Dan:

Correct coordinates, now!

*****

...Three

Two

One!

Nothing happened. Dan fumbled with the device. It appeared to have worked but where was Beth? A message flashed across his laptop screen. Thinking quickly, he addressed the board, "My apologies for the temporary glitch. My wife is the technical genius. I'm just the pretty face!"

It got a giggle from one of the ladies and a few smirks from the others. Good, he hadn't lost them. While smiling calmly at his audience, his fingers frantically hit the keyboard as he checked and sent the actual coordinates to Beth.

"Shall we try that again?" Dan giggled, cringing inwardly as he restarted the timer.

Three

Two

One…

There was a swirl of light behind him and suddenly Beth appeared. She stepped forward and took a bow.

"Ladies and gentlemen, I present to you, the world's first teleportation device."

The Cupcake Hustle

The art of the con, with a cake and a smile.

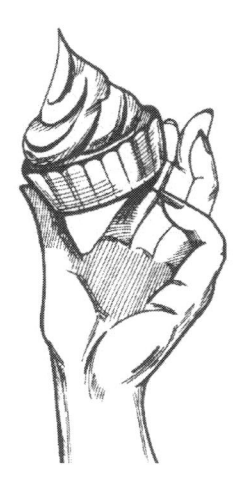

Joy was a most unlikely hustler, but beneath that innocent looking exterior lurked a shrewd and conniving mind. She painted on the first war paint of the day and admired the demure little housewife looking back out of the mirror. Smoothing the soft woollen cardigan over her tweed skirt, she smirked. Joy had planned this day meticulously, no detail left unchecked, from her loosely brushed hair right down to her sensible shoes. The list pinned to the kitchen noticeboard had every neatly penned item ticked off in a sparkly pink pen. Who would suspect this innocent-looking librarian of such a dastardly plan?

The excitement of what she was about to do bubbled up inside her. She knew she'd succeed; failure was not an option. She carefully balanced a huge box of cupcakes, iced with military precision, as she locked the front door. The game was on. Joy fixed her expression and strode boldly on to the first house.

Years of experience had taught her that brazen indifference worked best around these leafier suburbs. The cosseted inhabitants were totally unsuspecting as Joy worked her magic. They were ripe for the picking for an unscrupulous and devious mind. The key was to prey on their deepest fears, to exploit their vanity, greed, and pettiness. Con them with a smile and a cupcake!

The first house was always the hardest, but Joy had chosen well. A deliciously rich trophy wife with an aversion to the working class; perfect! She delighted in the revulsion on the Trophy Wife's face as she gingerly took the proffered cupcake, careful not to smudge her freshly manicured talons. Joy knew her cake would never add to the size six waistline. A shame really. Her strawberry frosting was quite delightful, but these were just necessary props in her master scam. Joy chuckled to herself as she brushed a few stray cat hairs from her skirt to the designer doormat. Disgust rising, Trophy Wife thrust some notes at Joy and slammed the door. Two crisp twenty-pound notes. Joy smiled as she folded them neatly into her cheap handbag. A small start, but something to build on. She would use this paltry offering to her advantage.

Joy remembered the dreary days of scruples and honesty as she made her way down the long, landscaped drive of the next victim. She recalled the days when the chink and rattle of coins had thrilled her. The days she would trawl the cheap local neighbourhood, being nice in exchange for a handful of loose change. Not so now. Her little white lies had gradually darkened as she left those futile scruples behind in the terraced streets. Why waste her precious time trudging round door to door? Those people didn't have the cash to spare and most just slammed the door against her polite requests. Joy had quickly realised the advantages to be gained if one was prepared to suppress the expected social niceties and embrace a life of deception.

Adrenaline now coursing through her veins, Joy composed her next hustle. Mansion number two, an ostentatious eyesore, held a fake-tanned, pampered princess. Joy delighted as she prepared to play on Pampered Princess' rivalry with the Trophy Wife next door; her research was paying off. Pitch expertly done, Pampered Princess was keen to outdo her neighbour any which way. Joy exchanged a pink frosted cupcake for an easy fifty pounds. Judging by the pudgy ankles squidged into her Manolo Blahniks, this was one cupcake that wouldn't be heading straight for the bin. Pampered Princess blatantly checked her watch and started to close the door. Her rude dismissal didn't go unnoticed, and Joy made a swift exit.

Joy took a moment to enjoy the view as she made her way to hustle number three. This beautiful countryside really was wasted on these madams who had more money than sense, and egos to match. The next house came into view, a showy glass-fronted affair, subtly mirrored to keep out prying eyes. Joy glanced round the manicured lawn, a playhouse and two very expensive looking blue tricycles - children! Joy rang the bell and winced at the tacky tune it played.

"Door!" a bored voice yelled from inside. Seconds later it was opened by a harassed-looking girl, two toddlers tussling around her feet. Joy started on her patter, taking in the scene. The overworked nanny shoed the boys out to the garden and sighed as she listened, probably glad to have a brief reprieve from the little monsters who were now fighting over a football. She glanced back nervously at her glitzy employer, who, phone in hand, was typing ferociously. Mistress Bling was dressed as only those who 'do lunch' do. An inappropriate amount of cleavage spilled over her tight, sparkly top. Her outfit screamed designer and no taste, and had no doubt cost more than Joy's entire wardrobe.

Joy waited patiently as Downtrodden Nanny crept in and whispered her request. Without a glance or a pause in her tweeting, she extracted a purse from the matching sparkly bag next to her and thrust it into Downtrodden Nanny's hand. Joy suppressed her grimace and replaced it with a conspiratorial grin as the nanny rolled her eyes and glanced back. Now the best bit, a cupcake in return for a couple of notes. Then, nodding at the squealing boys tearing round the lawn, she handed over another two cupcakes. Downtrodden Nanny hesitated, grinned, then grabbed another few twenties and thrust them back at an eager Joy.

"She'll never notice. Good luck!"

It was nearly time for lunch. Soon the BMWs with their personalised number plates would be heading out to the Village, their pristine owners strutting off to be seen in all the right places. Just time to visit a couple more houses before she paused for lunch herself. The homemade butties wrapped in foil were a far cry from the overpriced delicacies they would be nibbling.

Next stop, the residence of some local footballer. His celebrity status was wasted on Joy. She neither followed nor liked the game, but yet again, her homework had paid off.

His recent infidelities had earned him a sleazy reputation and a number of front-page headlines. Once Joy had convinced his long-suffering wife that she wasn't a reporter after a juicy story, she set about her task. Joy almost felt sorry for her, as she capitalised on the poor woman's need to make amends for her husband's rather public misdemeanours. With a weary smile, she handed over more than double the cash Joy had hustled so far. Another pink frosted cupcake turned into deliciously crinkly notes.

House after house, Joy adjusted her patter, exploited weaknesses, stroked egos, and capitalised on petty jealousies. A little flirtation with the leather-clad minx at the farmhouse yielded another fifty pounds and an invitation to return! A tasty morsel of fabricated gossip for the busty blonde at number thirty added an easy forty pounds, and her adoring, eyelash fluttering glances at the lecherous lout down the end of the lane were rewarded with a fan of twenties. Each hustle was individually crafted and most lucrative. Hours of research into the newly rich and wannabe famous were paying off. She revelled in her power to coerce the obscenely rich into handing over their pocket money. The crisp wad of folded notes crinkling under Joy's caress grew and grew.

Finally, her cupcake box was empty and her purse overflowing. Joy wiped a smear of pink frosting from the inside if the box and licked her fingers; it really was quite delicious. It had been a good day's work and such fun, but the best was yet to come.

Just time to nip home for a quick celebratory coffee and change into a more appropriate outfit: skinny jeans, high boots, and a casual jumper. She tossed her librarian persona into the wash basket and painted on a fresh face. A more hip and powerful Joy pouted back from the mirror. Cradling the heavy bag of cash, Joy locked the door and headed out once more.

The rest of the gang were already seated when Joy arrived. She wasn't late, Joy was never late, she just liked to hang back to maximise on making her entrance. One by one, the others emptied pockets and purses, adding to the disappointing pile of coins and small notes. It was a pathetic offering. Joy savoured the moment. It was time. Shoulders back, head held high, she triumphantly strode into the staffroom and placed the laden bag down on the coffee table, sending coppers rolling to the floor.

One thousand, three hundred and fifty lovely pounds!

Joy met the bemused stares of the other mums with a joyous grin. She pretended not to notice as they gaped at her ill-gotten gains, but secretly enjoyed her moment. The headmaster rubbed his hands with glee, eyes glistening as he mentally planned where he would spend the money. The children of Holly Leaf Primary would get their new books and play equipment, after all. And Joy, well, Joy could bask in the limelight, happy that she'd earned her rightful place as the Queen of the PTA mums.

Dwelling in the Shadows

A deadly pact forged with fear and love.

My life is good: a loving family, a respectable job, and a comfortable home. I want for nothing; I need nothing and yet a dark secret hides within me—a shadowy darkness wrapped up, bound, and camouflaged with a smile. Everything comes at a price.

I exist in the light of rainbows and laughter carried along on the magic of imagination. I don't do half measures with glasses, mine overflow with bubbles. I thrive on emotions and seek out the joy and sparkly enthusiasm in others, but even glitter has a darker side.

I wander deep amongst the trees, alone, safe in my isolation from prying eyes. I shed the sparkles and smiles. Naked, my soul laid bare, I peel away the layers of protection and allow the turmoil of emotions to seep through: anger, pain, regret, grief. Something whispers in the woods. A mere hint of a breeze chills my flesh. I pause and shudder, listening—nothing. Returning to my musings, I wince as memories, raw and recent, leak out. Harsh words spoken in anger and my heart aches for the hurt they caused to others. I sob for the hole ripped through my heart. I let these memories go, wishing them away, willing them to go. I send them out into the tangle of thorny brambles around my feet as a message—I am here.

A grey cloud of emotions oozes around my ankles then slowly seeps into the damp earth, seeking out its mistress.

Something stirs in the woods, the darkness between the distant trees deepens and draws closer as she awakens. I feel her presence like icy fingernails trailing down my spine. A shiver of revulsion follows her touch. I feel the watcher in the wood, and I know she feels me. I do not see her yet, but I know she's awake now. Watching and waiting. My feet are rooted in her cool moist earth, connecting us. She feeds on emotion. I need her yet fear her. I long to run, get away from this place, never to return, but her perverse anticipation washes over me, holding me captive. This is how it has to be.

I dig deeper, more purposeful now and feel the loss of beloved friends, those who made such an impact on my life, now gone. I wallow in self-pity and mourn my losses. Each tear, each last breath haunts my core, bringing new tears. They flow hot streams down my raw skin. Then chill. I let the realisations of my own mortality wash over me…the fear and pain of leaving behind my children to grow up motherless. Will this be the time? My heart wrenches at the thought.

A cool breeze circles, the cold descending as a cloud shields the sun. She's drawing closer now. I feel her icy talons reach out to pry open the darkness inside me. She watches the cycles of seasons and death as it returns to the soil. She watches the beauty and decay of her wilderness prison, yet she feels no joy nor sadness. She feeds on the stench of the rotting flesh as it brings forth new life. The watcher is here now. Her face close, putrid breath burns my throat as she sucks the fear and revulsion from me. Nauseated, I turn my face, but I can't escape the fetor of decay. Delighted, she drinks in my discomfort.

"More...." she hisses, her voice just an eerie whisper on the breeze. I remove the last flimsy layers, stretched tight over my biggest heartache. I remember my father and I cry hot silent tears of woeful grief. My shoulders shake as heavy sobs wrack my body, my knees weaken, and I sink to the woodland floor, foetal, exhausted. I remember grasping his frail hand as he took his last ragged breath, and the guilty feeling of relief that his pain had ended. She is enraptured as she gorges on the raw emotions seeping from my every pore, tearing into my heart, savouring the flavours of hurt, betrayal, guilt, and shame.

The watcher withdraws slightly, her spectral form slithers to the shadows. I gasp in a breath of clean air and slowly back away from her expressionless glare. She mirrors my steps, stops, and sniffs the air. A freakish smile splits her lips.

"More...." she rasps.

Drained, I shake my head. I have nothing more to give.

"More...." Her voice, like the sudden screech of a knife across a plate, vibrates through my skull. "Our deal...."

I screw my eyes tight, unwilling to revisit that memory. Though I can't see her, I feel her drawing closer again, her excitement rising as the stench of her breath cloys at my throat. I try to clear my head, think of anything but that day. I think of fluffy clouds drifting across a sapphire sky as the sun beats down on my face. But it was sunny that day too. I try to clear the picture that has risen in my mind. I can't bear to look.

She cackles, aware she has unlocked my deepest emotions, then she sighs in satisfaction. I can no longer block out what I've kept hidden for a whole season. That was the day that started everything, summoning forth my saviour and tormentor. As the tears stream down my face, the torturous scene replays.

*****

It's a gorgeous day for a walk in the woods. My daughter skips and dances through the ferns, stopping occasionally to pick up a pebble or feather. We pause each time to examine her treasures before they disappear into her pocket. Grubby fingers grasp mine as we explore far from the well-trodden path. We find a fabulous old tree; its boughs hang low to the ground, providing a little oasis of shade. I sit for a moment, my back resting against the gnarly trunk as my daughter scrambles up through the branches.

She's always been a climber, I muse, *I really should build her a treehouse in the garden.* I close my eyes for a moment, enjoying the peace...then suddenly I'm startled back to reality. The tearing screech of broken branches mingles with her screams...then thud.

I'm so close. I watch her fall. Time slows. I leap to catch her, but it's too late. Her tiny frame lays splayed over the rotten tree bough; legs bent at an unnatural angle. Her eyes stare glassily up to the blue sky and her red-soaked hair tangles with the brambles. I feel for a pulse, but I know it's too late. She's gone.

A raw anguish surges through me and freezes my senses. Inside, I'm screaming, sobbing, but I utter no sound. I feel the blackness fold over me, chilling my bones. Still rooted to the woodland floor, thorny stems ripping my skin, I watch the darkness take form. A wraith hangs over my daughter's broken body. I try to blink to clear my vision, but the wraith still shrouds my poor baby. I want to run, scream, tear it away, but I can do nothing but stare.

Slowly, the wraith turns to face me. She studies me and breathes in my anguish, entranced by the rush of emotion, she sighs with deep satisfaction.

"I can bring her back." The wraith's voice whispers through my head. I'm not thinking, just grasping onto those words, the only words I want to hear. I want my daughter back. I can't live without her. The wraith nods. I didn't speak, but she's accepted my decision.

"If I bring her back, you must replace what you have taken from me. As each season passes into the next, you must return to this place. You will feed me your fears, your anguish, your guilt, and your horror. This is our deal. Break the deal and I take back her soul. I am the watcher. I see all."

A swirl of fear, reluctance, and longing clouds my mind. I nod again. I need my daughter. I will do anything to save her. She leans in close, so close I can see the darkness behind her sunken eyes. Her rotting fingers grab my hair, holding me still, as she slowly licks my cheek. Her blackness weighs heavy on me. I'm drifting ….

"Mummy!" I'm startled awake by a little hand shaking my shoulder. "Silly Mummy, you fell asleep." She giggles as I draw her in for a hug. I bury my face in her hair and stroke her head, dreading to feel it slick with blood, but no, she's fine. She's perfect. She's alive. Did I just dream everything? My little girl wriggles out of my grasp and balances on a fallen branch. It's the branch, the one that didn't hold her weight.

 "Remember our deal…" The watcher's voice echoes through my head. "In one season …." Her last word blends with the breeze.

*****

I can take no more. Maybe this time she will renege on our deal, take more than my body can give. Will she drain me of every fibre that holds my soul together, leaving behind a dry husk of flesh and bones? She delights in this last surge of emotion, sipping the fear pulsing through my veins. I'm fading. The sounds of the woodland blur to static noise.

My eyes are open, but I see only darkness and its thick velvet cloak smothers me. Maybe it would be easier just to let go, to sink into the earth, my rotting corpse providing nutrients for new life. I accept my fate and a shiver of calm glints through the darkness. I feel her ragged tongue lick my cheek; her last act is a reminder of our agreement. A wave of revulsion shudders through me, but I know my ordeal has ended, for now. The inky cloak of darkness slides over me and slinks back into the trees. She won't let me go that easily. I have survived to live another season. I wait, breath held, as she silently slithers back into the darkest recesses of the forest, sated until my return.

The sun's warm rays caress my back as I let out a final silent scream. I shake off the self-pity and remember instead the kind words that brought smiles and healing hugs. I remember a childhood of laughter and recall my father's wise words. He taught me to live life and love life. Slowly, I uncurl as the last wisps of my own darkness retreat back inside, lighter, more bearable. The layers of self-preservation fold over the hurt, wrapping it deep within, sealing the wound. My body calms, and my dried tears sparkle through fresh eyes as I soak up the healing force of nature. I think of my daughter waiting to be picked up from school, and smile. Renewed, I step out of my shadows and back into the sunshine. You can't truly appreciate the light if you've never dwelled in the shadows.

For Sale

A mysterious house and a dose of curiosity.

The For Sale sign hung wonkily outside the faded grey house. It was strange she'd never noticed it before, despite driving past many times, she thought. But it was awkwardly squeezed between two well-kept, bigger houses, and set a little further back from the road. She'd only noticed it because she'd stopped to post a letter. She turned back to gaze at the house, wondering what kind of person would buy it. *It's a bit rundown,* she mused, *but nothing a little paint and hard work won't fix. I wonder what the interior is like.*

Curiosity took over. She was looking to downsize, and she had some time to kill. A little look round would satisfy her nosiness and maybe this would turn out to be the ideal house for her. Since the children had grown up and moved out, she'd been feeling lost in their large family home.

Decision made, she stepped through the rickety gate and carefully made her way up the uneven cobbled path. She raised her fist to knock, but before she made contact, the door creaked open on ancient hinges.

"Shall I give you the tour?" A soft, whispery voice came from inside.

She paused as a chill spiralled up her spine. Her curiosity wrestled with the strange feeling of unease, but she shook it off. The voice had created a picture of an old woman in her mind, nothing to worry about…. Peering through the open doorway, revealed a carved oak staircase, and an empty room with dusty floorboards. Cobwebs festooned the peeling frame of the far window. *Perhaps this will be too much work,* she pondered, but it would be rude to walk away now, and she was fascinated to see the rest of the house.

She stepped in through the door and looked for the old woman. "I'd love a tour," she called into the gloom inside. "But where are you?"

"I'm right here beside you." The speaker, still hidden, laughed nervously. "I'm sorry, we're not used to your sort here."

"My sort? What do you mean, 'my sort'?"

"Forgive my rudeness, dear, but we're not used to the living on this side of the veil, but you're very welcome to step through."

Cake Roulette

Perfection is in the planning.

Barbara had been holding the crime writers' group for a number of years now. Members had come and gone over the years, but the group remained a vibrant hive of ideas, as well as a good opportunity for her to sell her latest novels. Once a week, the new writers turned up eager to share snippets of their latest stories, then soak up the expert advice from their award-winning local author. Some of the stories were a little tedious, but she always tried to give positive feedback. This group would never make it to publication. Still, it was quite relaxing to sit around discussing the perfect murder over a cup of tea and a slice of cake.

The secret to her success was in the planning; her readers would never know the hours of research that went into her crime novels, but it was an essential part of the process. Barbara was quite a stickler for the details. "There's no point in writing something that could be proved inaccurate," she often said to her group. "Plan, research, and check even the smallest details—even fiction needs a grounding in truth to be believable." It was quite clear from their readings that her group were more dedicated to the cake and social chitchat than doing the research required to be a serious author.

These wannabe authors expect to become an instant success without any of the hard work, she mused as she busied herself in the kitchen, baking for this afternoon's meeting. She flicked back and forth between her laptop and preparing the refreshments, multitasking research for her new book, as she measured, beat, and stirred the cake mixture. Today she was researching aconite, also known as wolfsbane or devil's helmet. *Hmmm, such a beautiful flower, but deliciously deadly*, she thought. It was an ideal murder weapon for her new protagonist.

"As little as 2 mg of aconite or 1g of the plant may cause death from respiratory paralysis or heart failure... death occurs within two to six hours in fatal cases. The only post-mortem signs are those of asphyxia," she read out loud as she spooned the mixture into cake cases—pretty floral ones for the guests, and plain white for her own gluten-free version. *Hmm, plenty of time for my character to distance himself from the victim, and it's undetectable too. 'Very handy!'* she thought, mentally planning out the first chapter.

The smell of freshly baked cakes wafted through the house as she opened the door to welcome in the group. Taking it in turns, they each read their flash fiction story inspired by the theme set the previous week. Soon it was time to bring out the tea and cakes. Placing her own cake to one side, she arranged the rest on a large china plate—they looked so pretty with the swirls of purple blue icing on top—then carried them through to the lounge.

She wondered who would be helping with her book research today.

"Cake anyone?"

Sweet Solitude

Embracing the calm.

It's amazing how quickly a mug of coffee next to a campfire can soothe away the stresses of life. I gaze absentmindedly around my woodland paradise; the deep green pine needles still cling to their branches, but the chestnut leaves now form a soft golden carpet under my feet. A harsh cry stirs me from my reverie, and I look up. The bare tree branches create windows to view a cloudless sky as I search for the source of noise. A buzzard circles overhead, calling to its mate. They meet, circle once more, then in perfect unison, they dive, lost from view below the treeline.

I sit back in my chair and savour another mouthful of coffee. Its rich aroma mingles with the scent of damp pine and the wood smoke, rejuvenating me. The breeze through the leaves clears my mind and my breathing slows to the rhythm of the swaying branches. I feel my troubles dropping away like the autumn leaves.

It's beautiful here in my own isolated little woodland, silent once again, no pressure, nothing to do but sip my coffee and ponder while I stare into the flickering flames. I gaze, hypnotised by the fiery dance amongst the blackened sticks. They lick at the cloth and flare bright crimson, hissing as the fire consumes the evidence of my endeavours.

I grimace slightly as the act of raising my mug jars my aching shoulder. It's a good ache though, a sign of a job well done. I'll sleep well tonight. I lean forward, the heat of the blaze warms my chilled skin. Finally, I drain the mug and watch as the fire reduces the blood-stained clothing to nothing but a pile of ashes. The fresh earth clinging to the spade at my feet is the only reminder now. I sigh into the breeze and breathe in the contentment of newfound solitude.

Scents on the Breeze

A penny for the guy.

The smell of black peas and spiced mulled wine wafted on the cool autumn breeze. Most of the villagers, and some outsiders, milled around in the dark, sipping the hot drink or cradling a tub of the traditional bonfire night supper. The children, wrapped up in big coats, hats and wellies, waved sparklers from gloved hands, marvelling as they attempted to write their names in the chilly air before the glow disappeared.

Lined up behind the safety cordon, five small groups stood, making the final adjustments to the life-sized guys they'd created—no longer a 'penny for the guy', the prize was a considerable amount more and the prestige of lighting the bonfire. Each group was determined to win it. The judges on the Shady Acres bonfire committee made their way slowly along the line of competition entrants chatting with each group. There was an obvious winner, but they deliberately gave equal time to each group of eager teens proudly presenting their guy.

The bonfire was set. It just needed a prize-winning guy to sit on the top. The judges nodded to one another and made their way back to the winning pair. Their guy had a spooky carved pumpkin face, peeping out through a balaclava, and the judges had agreed that this extra effort deserved the prize.

Dave and Martin grinned and pocketed their fifty quid prize money, then carefully hoisted their guy up onto the woodpile. Martin held it in place, wedging the body between two planks of wood, and sneakily squirted lighter fuel over its clothing. Dave adjusted the scary pumpkin face, worried it would slip off before the flames took over, but they knew it would be quickly engulfed in flames.

The committee did a last check to make sure no children had strayed under the barrier, then gave the signal to Dave and Martin to light the bonfire. The lads made their way round the pile of old planks and dry sticks, lighting the scrumpled wads of newspaper between. The bonfire caught quickly, and a cheer went up from the crowd.

The lads grinned, high fived each other and shot each other a knowing look. Mission accomplished, they ducked back under the ropes and stood for a moment just staring at the flames, bright orange against the black sky. They watched in silence with the crowd until the fire reached their guy. It flashed brightly as the lighter fuel caught and the guy was quickly engulfed in plumes of black spiralling smoke.

"Job done!" Dave whispered.

"Yep. Drink?" Martin nodded towards the drinks tent. They wandered back, weaving through families huddled together, avoiding children munching on sticky toffee apples, and made their way to the bar to spend their winnings.

"Well done, lads. That was a very lifelike guy you had there, and scary too." The mayor of Shady Acres raised his glass to the lads and nodded to the guy, now blazing scarlet against the dark sky. "But weren't there three of you here originally?"

Martin spluttered into his beer.

"Oh, he's here somewhere," Dave said with a sly wink to his mate.

"Yeah, he's probably just enjoying the bonfire," Martin agreed.

The flaming guy collapsed into the glowing embers in the centre of the bonfire. A smell similar to that of roast pork, and wood smoke mingled with the black peas and mulled wine spices wafting on the autumn breeze.

Trick or Treat?

Dare you risk it?

The chocolate shop bell tinkled as she bustled through the door, hugging her warm woollen coat close to avoid knocking over the tantalising displays.

"Good timing. I was just about to close up for the night. How can I help you?"

The woman gazed at the vast array of handmade chocolates in a Halloween box. Dark chocolates iced with pumpkins, skulls, and coffins, caught her eye.

"Hmm, there's so much choice, and they all look delicious."

"Can I offer you a go on my Trick or Treat roulette?" said the chocolatier as he reached under the counter for a silver platter. "They may look the same, but each one is as unique as you and me. Choose a treat and you can pick any box free of charge."

"And if I get a trick…?" she queried.

"Well, tricks for some, are treats for others." The old man grinned as he pushed the platter towards her.

The lady returned his grin. Never one to pass up a freebie, she leant forward to inspect the chocolates. Just behind the counter, she spotted a pile of folded clothing. It looked incongruous next to the carefully crafted displays.

The chocolatier followed her gaze. "Been collecting clothes for the homeless. Going to take it down to the shelter tomorrow."

"Ah," she nodded, smiling, and made her choice.

The chocolate instantly melted in her mouth. "Mmm, delicious…" She bit down to taste the centre. A feeling of euphoria flooded her body. The chocolatier watched in glee for her reaction. "I got a treat," she tried to say, but the words wouldn't form. The feelings of bliss simmered to a hazy calm, then nothing. "I got tricked!" was her final thought as she faded from reality.

The chocolatier watched as the lady's body dissolved until only a wisp of smoke remained. It swirled from the bundle of clothes she once wore, and dissipated in the cool October air. He reached into the clothing, drew out a chocolate and placed it in the space on the silver platter. Then, carefully, he folded the woollen coat, and added it to the pile of clothes behind the counter.

"Tricks for some are treats for others," he chuckled, and locked up the shop for the night.

Great North Western

Enjoy the journey!

Welcome to Great North Western Trains. We aim to make your journey as comfortable as possible. With that in mind, please avoid the toilet in coach D. Seriously, you DO NOT want to go in there! There are other toilets located in coaches A and G, but be advised, you will need to take your own loo roll.

Feel free to place your bags on the spare seat next to you. The other paying passengers really won't mind standing in the aisles, but watch they don't trip you on your way out.

Overpriced coffee and stale cakes are available in the buffet car in coach B. For those in coach G, don't bother! You'll never make it back to your seat without scalding yourself.

The trolley service will be shortly making its way down the train. Those wearing open-toed sandals, please be aware that train insurance no longer covers broken toes. Passengers in coach A planning to disembark at Stockport are advised to set off now. You won't stand a chance of making it to the door once the trolley sets off.

Please note that Coaches F and G are quiet zones. Passengers are permitted to frown disapprovingly at the businessman in the shiny suit who is currently on the phone bragging about his latest sales figures. And also, at the lady in the blue dress, whose headphones are not plugged in.

Great North Western welcomes travellers of all ages and is keen to be of service. Children should feel free to run off any excess energy up and down the aisles. Mums, make yourselves comfortable, put your feet up on the seat in front—we don't mind a bit of mud on our upholstery. Any unattended toddlers can be collected from the lost-property office in Manchester at the end of the week.

We are now approaching Stockport. When leaving, please remember to take your luggage with you. The bins are no doubt full, so feel free to leave your sticky sweet wrappers and empty cups on the floor near your seat—the cleaners appreciate being kept in a job.

Thank you for enduring Great North Western Trains, and as you leave, please mind the gap between your expectations and reality.

Coming Out of my Shell

Enduring the bully.

'Workplace Bullying', the words boldly glared out from the leaflet a colleague slipped into my hand. I quickly shoved it into my handbag, just having it was causing my cheeks to flush.

"A few of us are considering taking action," Suze whispered, subtly flicking her eyes towards the tyrant in question. I followed her gaze; the feeling of dread and loathing flooded my body as I took in the false smile plastered across the face I'd come to hate. She was tapping her false nails on the desk as she waited impatiently for the last few people to take a seat.

My heartbeat quickened as I considered what taking action might mean. But workplace bullying? I'm an adult, children get bullied, not forty-year-olds in a professional environment. It sounded ludicrous to call it that, but what was it? Constantly being asked to cover for others during my admin time, then being in trouble for being behind on my admin work? What about being missed off team emails and not being informed about 'compulsory' meetings, which (deliberately?) took place on my only afternoon off? Then there were the times she'd singled out people in meetings to berate them—was this bullying?

I dreaded these meetings, the ones I was informed about. The feeling of creeping dread would take over as I waited for it to be my turn to be in the firing line. It was inevitable that moment would arrive, however hard I worked. But taking action? Would I dare to speak up against her? Doing so would paint an even bigger target on my back. Maybe if there were enough of us willing to speak out....

"Jane! Stand up!"

Her sneering snarl cut through my musing. My heart thudded, flooding my cheeks with beetroot red. Tentatively, I rose on jelly legs.

"You can go first with your presentation, seeing as you're obviously bored."

Presentation? What presentation?

"But of course you can't because you didn't attend my meeting yesterday. It was about staff slacking off and not pulling their weight—that sound familiar, Jane?"

The last words were spat out, then replaced with a smirk. Yes, this was bullying. All around, colleagues looked on, some embarrassed, some sending sympathetic glances.

"You can stay late to work on your presentation. Now sit back down."

I shrank back into my seat, humiliated. Suze surreptitiously patted my leg under the table—a silent show of support. Then something snapped inside me. She WAS a bully, and I'd had enough. I swallowed down the rising nausea and stood up...

"No, Joanne," I cut her off as she'd started on her next victim. A collective gasp filled the silence, and all eyes turned to see Joanne's ugly, incredulous glare.

"I beg your pardon! I told you to sit," she snarled ferociously.

"I have my presentation ready, and I am quite prepared to deliver it now," I snarled back at her, years of pent-up frustration bubbled to the surface. "It's on workplace bullying. It's about cruel bosses who treat their staff unfairly—that sound familiar, Joanne?"

Dark and Stormy Night

Braving the storm alone.

It was a dark and stormy night... Only a fool would be camping out in weather like this, but here I am, with only a thin canvas sheet between me and the raging elements.

Damn you, smiley weather man—you lied to me! You promised me sunshine and clear skies for my first solo camp. My idyllic musings of yesterday, plans of relaxing at my campfire, listening to the peaceful song of the woodlands being washed away in the downpour. I guess the sensible thing would be to pack up and go home, but it was hard enough wrestling my way out of soaking clothes, trying desperately to minimise the flood in the tent, while the airbed conspired to bounce me back out into the storm. No, I'm not leaving my dry haven until the smiley weather man makes good on his promise.

I'm hungry. The meal I'd planned to cook remains a pile of raw ingredients in a cooler bag. Instead, my tea was the chocolate bar I packed for a late-night snack. At least I'm warm, though. I pull my sleeping bag tighter around my shoulders and snuggle into the airbed—it's ceased trying to eject me from the tent. I guess warm and hungry is better than cold, wet, and hungry, but I'd kill for a bacon butty right now.

Snuggled in my cocoon, I listen to the beat of the raindrops. The wind whipping through the branches adds the melody to the watery percussion—my own forest concert—a little night music. The timbre changes. It builds, intensifies until it reaches its crescendo, then settles back to a gentle melody of leaves dancing through the drops. My mind drifts with the rhythm of the rain.

I don't know what woke me; I don't even remember falling asleep. I remember listening to the storm…that's what's different—it's quiet. Maybe the absence of noise was what woke me. My tummy rumbles. I squint at my phone to see the time—5am. Too early for breakfast? My tummy growls in disagreement. Clumsily, I pull on dry clothes and clamber out of my tent. It's still dark, but this is my solo camp, my rules, and there's nobody to tell me it's a ridiculous time for breakfast.

After a few failed attempts (and much swearing) the fire lights, and it's not long before the kettle is boiling, and the eggs and bacon are sizzling in the pan. I sit back with my coffee, proud of my efforts. The storm has cleansed the woodland and scented the breeze: cool pine and damp earth mingles with wood smoke and the delicious aromas of my long-awaited meal. Oh, that smell…I'm practically drooling into the campfire.

Finally, with a full tummy, I join the birds to welcome in the new day. The first golden hues sparkle through the raindrops as the sun slowly pushes the darkness away. I breathe in the beauty and give silent thanks to the thunderstorm, which led me to this perfect moment.

Framed

The magic beyond.

Legend says, you don't find a hag stone; it finds you. And this one certainly found me. As I settled down on the cool sand to watch the sun setting over the ocean, the smooth pebble nestled into my palm. It fit perfectly. I gently blew the sand away to reveal a round hole, just big enough to fit my little finger.

I dredged through my memory as I held the pebble up to peer through it. Waves crashed upon the shore beneath my feet, the foam glowing golden under the sinking sun. The magic had something to do with water… I squinted through the hole, trying to remember the folklore as I tracked the sun's descent. That was it, the flow of water creating the hag stone's hole, also created a magical passage that only allowed goodness to flow through and kept out evil. A lucky stone then.

I smiled and lowered the hag stone, following the sinking sun so it remained framed in the centre. The sunset painted the clouds with shades of amber and flame against the darkening sky. I watched as the scarlet sun settled onto distant waves and another memory floated to the surface. A hag stone was supposed to allow its owner a glimpse into the faerie realms.

I peered purposely through the hole but saw only the beauty of the sun disappearing beyond the horizon—no faerie folk flitting across the sky, no enchanted lands rising out of the ocean. Disappointed, I lowered the hag stone to take in the last fiery glows. Maybe I've grown too old to see into faerie realms. I dropped the stone into my pocket and marvelled as a blanket of indigo settled over the sea.

I stuck my hand back in my pocket, absentmindedly tracing the stone's hole with my finger. Perhaps the magic always exists for those who take the time to see it. Maybe I don't need a hag stone to see into the faerie realms after all. I returned the hag stone to the sand for someone else to claim. I had all the beauty I needed right here.

Naughty Step

Time out for a break.

I'm on the naughty step again! I didn't mean to shout, but they were bugging me. They'd been bugging me all morning, and nobody cares! One minute of punishment for each year of my age. That's the rule, isn't it? I'm not sure I'll last that long!

It's so unfair! I mean, it's not even my mess all over the floor—I didn't knock over the box of Lego, and it wasn't me who crushed cake crumbs into the new rug. It wasn't me who brought down a million cuddly toys from the bedroom for a tea party.

They were being particularly horrible today, and to be honest, I'd rather be here than downstairs right now, with them. Here is tidy and peaceful. It's a flipping mess down there; let them deal with it for once! Let them sweep up the glitter sparkling on the rug. Let them mop up the spilt cup of juice that's slowly trickling under the sofa. They haven't even noticed it. They won't though...

I'd tell them to clear up the mess, but nobody listens to me—until I shout. I don't like shouting. Shouting is what put me on the naughty step.

I can hear them yelling at each other. Occasionally my name is called, repeated—over and over. I delight in ignoring them for once. I can see them clearly, but I'm invisible to them on the naughty step—thank goodness!

I watch as cushions get thrown; they sparkle with the glitter from the rug and, actually, it looks quite pretty from up here. Little glitter mushroom clouds poof up into the air, slowly settling to sparkle the surfaces that escaped the original mess.

Just a few more minutes. Then I'll have to go down and face them. The urge to shout has gone; timeout really does work. I feel much calmer now and ready to deal with whatever ordeals lie ahead. Ah well, deep breath, one…two…three… Happy face back on. I suppose it's time to go back to being the perfect patient parent!

Note to self: next time bring a coffee.

Her at Number 7

Revenge is sweet.

I never did like her at number 7, not since she gave me that awful reading, not to mention her condescending reassurance that she was sure I would be able to overcome 'difficulties' ahead of me—smug cow! The only difficulties I have are living next door to her. I'm quite content being single, and I enjoy living alone. Thank you very much, Gloria.

Oh wow, another car of cops has turned up, or are they forensics? It's hard to tell from up here with that tree in the way. Still, I've got a few good photos for the local Facebook group… Hmmm, I wonder if I can see better through the spare room window?

That's better. I can see everything now. Oh, what a shame, Gloria, they're digging up your precious roses… guess you won't be bragging about winning first prize at the show this year. It serves you right! You always did think you were better than the rest of us with that fancy boyfriend, half your age—where is he now, eh Gloria? You don't know, but I do!

Blimey, they're making a lot of mess. I'm so glad it's not my garden they're digging up. Ooh, that's a good shot, the look on your face…that's definitely going on Facebook later, it'll go viral. Come on Mr. Policeman, dig to the left a bit…just a little more…got it!

That crime-scene tape frames the pic perfectly—another great shot of your demise, eh Gloria? Not so posh now are you, being dragged away in handcuffs for all the neighbourhood to see?

*****

I had to commend myself on such a genius plan, though to be fair, I didn't set out to do this. It just kind of happened. Xander, had come round to say goodbye and ask me to give Gloria a note. Before I could ask why, the poor lad burst into tears, so I ushered him in to make him a cup of tea. In between sobs he told of how he'd tried to leave her several times, but she'd begged him to stay, laying on the emotional blackmail so thickly he felt stifled. Poor lad didn't know what to do, so now he was taking the easy route and sneaking off, while Gloria was visiting her mother. If she'd been a nicer person, I'd have felt sorry for her, but I had to agree with Xander, this was the easiest way out.

Xander perked up a bit as he justified his reasons for leaving her—and none of it surprised me! I brought out a cake to cheer him up and handed him a knife to cut himself a slice, but he fumbled and sliced his finger, gushing blood all over his plate. Xander apologised profusely while I bandaged his finger, but I barely listened as an idea was started to take form. I carefully moved the bloody plate to the side—it would come in useful later once he was safely out of the way—and got him a clean one. Now, Xander was conveniently lying low in London, having secured a new job far away from his domineering ex.

*****

Well, that was entertaining. Time for a cuppa, I think, while I post these pics. Ooh, I can just imagine the news tomorrow:

'Local Psychic Arrested

Following an anonymous tip off, police have discovered a blood-stained weapon buried in the backyard of psychic, Gloria Day. An investigation into the suspicious disappearance of her tomboy lover is ongoing…'

There's always a way to "overcome difficulties", Gloria—bet you didn't see this in your reading, did you?

Breadsticks and Custard Slices

An accidental hero.

"Look who it is! The hero of the hour." Roy shouted as Gerald strode proudly through the door of the Black Dog pub.

"Oy, Gerry, you too famous to sit with us now?" Bill added with a laugh. "You made the front page of The Horwich Gazette!"

His mates clapped him on the back and heckled as Gerald settled into his usual pub seat.

"Buy us a pint and I'll tell you the tale…" Gerald waited until he had gathered an audience, took a mouthful of the Guinness he'd just been handed, then grinned.

"As you know, our Brenda is rather partial to a custard slice with a cup of tea, so sends me t' get her custard slices and a breadstick from that new bakery on the high street. I'd just set off home, when, BAM! This scruffy lout comes running full pelt across the road and slams straight into me—I nearly lose me footing and think, 'oh shit, I'm going down,' but suddenly, I'm jerked up again…"

"What'd you do, Gez?" Bill butted in.

"Well, I don't even have time to shout. Next thing, I'm being dragged along—the handle of my bag's caught on the kid's jacket buckle.

'Oy, STOP!' I yell. But do you know what that cheeky oik shouts? *'Bog off, granddad!'* Can you believe it?"

Gerald stopped for a gulp of Guinness, nodding as his drinking companions muttered and murmured about the youth of today.

"No respect for their elders, these young uns!" Roy grumbled from behind his half pint of lager. "Go on, what happened next?"

"Well, he shoves me and keeps on running. I have no choice but to follow. I'm still attached and being dragged along. Custard's oozing through the bag, breadcrumbs are flying everywhere… I'm thinking how much trouble I'll be in from our Brenda if her slices get smushed. I grab the breadstick and whack him round the head!"

"Good on yer, Gez!" Bill cheered.

Another gulp of Guinness…Gerald paused to savour the moment, as half the pub was now listening in.

"He goes straight down, pulling me down on top of him—there's custard everywhere! I'm sitting on top of the lout trying to get my breath back and untangle my bag, while he's shouting…well, I daren't repeat it. A bunch of kids come running over, and I can't have language like that in front of the little uns, so I whack him again to shut him up…. And that's when the cops show up.

"Turns out, Scruffy Lout just robbed the corner shop— emptied the till and legged it with a load of cash, a box of cigs and a king-sized Mars Bar. And in my mission to save Brenda's custard slices, I'd single-handedly apprehended the thieving little git."

Gerald paused to gulp a few mouthfuls of his pint as his mates cheered and chortled.

"What happened next, Gerry?" Even Barry the barman had wandered over to listen.

"Well, everyone comes out cheering my heroic capture, then this young copper wanders over and grabs me…"

"What the hell?"

"And? Go on," Roy urged.

Gerald smirked as he got ready to deliver his groan-worthy punchline.

"Now, we're both in custardy and I'm done for assault with a breadly weapon!"

Number Five

Echoes of the past.

Five has always been my favourite number, a lucky number even. It was this thought that made me smile, as I counted aloud my steps into the woods - 553, 554, 555...ouch! I bumped into something hidden in the long ferns. Brushing aside leafy fronds revealed a half-buried stone. It looked like a long-since toppled gatepost, but it now served as a convenient seat to nurse my bruised toes. I ran my hand over the soft moss onto the cool stone and felt slight indentations. Peeping out from behind a mossy clump was a carving of sorts, so worn by time it was hard to make out. I brushed away the dirt—a five! It looked like a five and flowers, maybe some letters.

Gateposts signified an entrance to something more exciting, but where? I'd tramped through these woods many times and I had never seen any houses. I looked around. The woodland floor was thigh high in foliage, but there did seem to be a long gap through the trees—*could it be an overgrown path?*

I paused momentarily. *Would Mum mind me going so far?* The anticipation of adventure won, and I waded through, careful to avoid the thorny brambles. The dense thicket suddenly opened into a bright clearing, and there, hidden in the woods, was a wonky old cottage. Fragrant wild roses wove around trellises surrounding a blue wooden door, its number 5 glinting in the sunshine, and roses carved into the stone lintel intertwined with letters—5 Rose Cottage. I was just about to go have a closer look…

"Tea time! Come back now!"

Mum's voice echoed through the trees. Torn between investigating the mysterious hidden cottage and being in trouble for being late for tea, I took a last look. I turned away reluctantly, but reassured myself that I would definitely return another day.

***

I never did find my way back to Rose Cottage. I was so sure I would remember the way through the avenue of trees, but despite retracing my steps down the trampled path of brambles, the cottage had mysteriously vanished. Sadly, I returned to the gatepost and sat, disappointed. *I definitely didn't imagine it!*

My fingers traced the number 5 and gently scraped off the moss around it. Brushing away more of the moss and soil clinging to the cold stone, more roses and letters emerged from under years of mossy growth. Finally, I cleared the full length of the post, and stared as the realisation kicked in. It wasn't a gatepost after all, but the rose-carved lintel of Number 5 Rose Cottage.

Memory

The art of forgetting.

"Oh hello, Love. Nice of you to ring, but I can't stay chatting. I've got loads to do today." Elsie explained, thinking of the large piece of cake she was going to eat while watching Bargain Hunt.

"No problem, Mum. I was just checking you'd remembered I was coming round for lunch later."

Lunch? Dammit, I'd totally forgotten. What can I make for lunch?

"Of course I remembered, Darling. Must go. I'll see you later."

How did I forget Marie was coming? I'm sure I wrote it on the calendar....

Elsie wandered into the kitchen to check the calendar, just as the kettle boiled. She put the calendar down on the counter and silenced the noisy kettle. Marie had bought her a whistling kettle to remind her she'd put it on to make a cup of tea.

Ooh yes, a nice cup of tea...I could do with a nice cup of tea. I wonder if I have any cake to go with it?

Elsie grabbed her favourite china cup and went to get the milk. She spotted the calendar on the counter.

Ooh, I wonder why I left that there...what day is it today?

She put the cup and milk down and wandered back into the living room.

Date? I can find out from my phone. Now where are my glasses?

Elsie wandered back into the kitchen, adding the phone to the pile on the counter while she checked the cupboards for her glasses. They were never where she thought she'd left them. She checked in the cake tin....

Ooh cake. I'd forgotten about that. I'll have that in a minute. Now what was I looking for? Ah yes, the date. TV...It'll be on the TV...ooh Bargain Hunt will be on in a minute. I was just about to watch it when Marie rang....

The knock at the front door startled her out of her musing.

"Hi Mum. You didn't forget I was coming, did you?"

"Me forget? Of course not, Marie Darling. The kettle's just boiled and there's a lovely piece of cake for us on the counter."

Lucky Fifty

A lost coin.

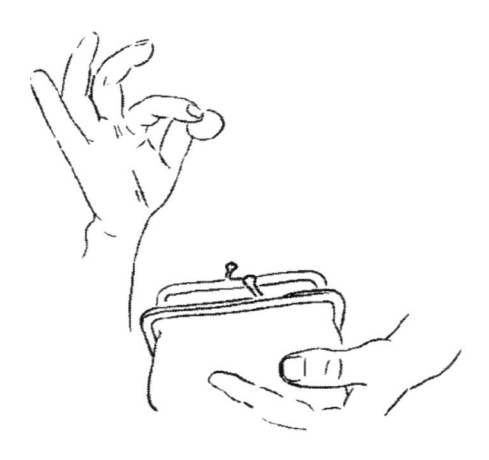

It appeared in a handful of change on my fiftieth birthday—a fiftieth anniversary fifty pence piece.

The repetition of fifty seemed too significant to ignore, and I adopted it as my lucky coin. It sat in the bottom of my purse, never to be spent, but there to bring a smile whenever I handed out pocket money to my girls.

"Mum, I'm off to Cadets now," my daughter called through to the kitchen where I was chopping veggies. "I grabbed some change from your purse…see you later."

I heard the rattle of dropped keys, the clatter of things being knocked over in her hasty exit, then I winced as the door slammed loudly. *That child's a walking disaster.* I chuckled to myself thinking about the wake of destruction she'd no doubt left—then her words registered…. *Change from my purse!* I ran to the front room; my purse was left open on the table-empty! My lucky fifty pence had gone.

I pulled open the door, already knowing she was long gone. I was right, the street was empty. Sadly, I closed the door, and picked up the boots and bags she'd knocked over in her hasty exit, replacing the dumped keys on the hook. I grabbed the purse to put it back in my handbag, and checked again, hoping to see my lucky fifty pence, but as expected, it wasn't there.

It's only a coin. It doesn't really matter, I told myself sadly as I shuffled back towards the kitchen. *If it's meant to be, it'll find its way back to me.*

My toe caught something. It skittered across the wooden floor, bounced off the skirting board and sat, glinting in the shadows—*could it be...?* My lucky 50p had found its way back. As I put my treasured fifty away safely, I gave silent thanks for having a clumsy child. It clearly was meant to be my lucky coin.

The Blank Canvas

Capturing the memories.

The blank canvas glared back accusingly, blinding white in the afternoon sun.

"Don't stare at the blank page, make your mark, any mark, then let the creativity flow through your brushes." She heard the whispered voice of her old teacher break through as she searched her memories for inspiration. Swishing the brush across the palette, she gathered shades of cobalt and indigo, making her mark. The paint swirled across the damp paper, rippling over the textured surface. No real purpose, just a splash of colour waiting for inspiration to give it direction. Brush clean, she selected a silvery blue. A quick flick of the bristles and a myriad of stars speckled across the blue.

She closed her eyes and allowed the colours to guide her thoughts. The shush of distant waves played a soundtrack to the splash of blue from the canvas. A memory surfaced….

*****

Little legs sprinting ahead, down a grassy path. A quick glance back to her parents' reassuring nods, she continued, hands outstretched, feeling the feathery grasses tickling her palms. The excitement of discovery spurred her on, the call of the sea, the cool sand beneath her toes, a deserted, moonlit beach....

Soft sand turned to smooth pebbles, slowing her descent. Carefully stepping from rock to rock as she reached the shore. Shells mingled with the shingle, a million shiny gifts from the sea. She paused, searching for the perfect treasure. 'Just one or two,' she heard her mother's constant reminder running through her mind. 'You can't bring every shell home with you.'

A wave rushed forward, rippling around her toes, and shifting the shingle beneath her feet. She delighted in the feeling as it rolled back into the dark water. The movement shuffled the shells, pushing new ones to the surface. Quickly she grabbed a shiny pink conch shell, shimmering in the moonlight—a mermaid shell, the perfect treasure. She'd be able to listen to the song of the sea in the shell and remember long after this moment passed.

She spun around, taking in the whole scene: the dark ocean, the indigo sky glittered with stars, the sand, and the grassy path. Then, pausing in wonder, she gazed across to their holiday home, perched on the edge of the world, in splendid isolation. And in that moment, she felt truly free, like the whole universe was hers to hold.

*****

Eyes open, she moved quickly, allowing the creativity to flow. Her brush danced across the canvas with the sunbeams. It was a race now, to recreate the picture before it floated away on the salty breeze. And finally, she laid the brush to rest next to a treasured memory captured in paint.

The Scent of Pine

Stealing the Christmas feast.

Alfie sniffed the air. The familiar earthy scent of pine coming from next door tingled his nostrils. He sighed with relief and smiled; he would eat well for the next few weeks.

It was Alfie's father who'd taught him that the arrival of the tree meant food in abundance. Dad was gone now, but Alfie cherished memories of sneaking into the neighbour's house together to feast on the biscuits, fruit, nuts and chocolates they left out on glittery surfaces.

Alfie's tummy rumbled at the thought of sweet, sugary treats. Patience would yield a much bigger haul of goodies, enough to last for weeks if he was clever. He couldn't risk being caught; it was better to wait…

Finally, the tree was sparkling, and branches hung low to the ground, weighed down with shiny things that twinkled in the lights. Best of all were the ones wrapped in crinkly paper. These held delicious creamy surprises, that gave him super-speed energy.

Alfie checked the room was clear, then crept quietly in. He had learned to first look at where everything was to make future raiding trips quicker and safer. *Nuts and fruit on the table, biscuits on the mantelpiece, shiny wrappers on the tree—lots of them!* He allowed himself a moment to taste a couple, then grabbed all he could and darted back next door.

The next few days followed the same pattern, and Alfie's stash of sugary contraband grew. He felt slightly guilty that next door's littlest child was getting blamed for his thieving, but Alfie stayed focused on his bountiful task.

Finally, the scent of pine was masked by a million different tantalising smells. The big feast day was finally here! Hidden from view by the piles of crumpled paper under the tree, Alfie scampered across the floor and took up his position under the table, ready to capture falling food. His long whiskers twitched in anticipation – Christmas was just the best time to be a mouse.

Tick Tock

Modern-day priorities.

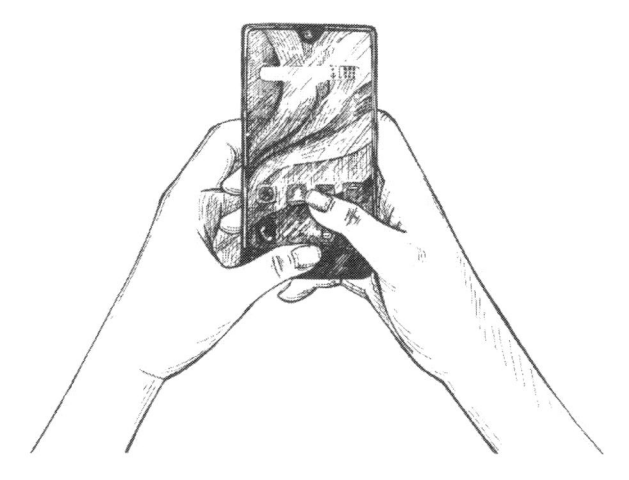

"Chloe, is that you at the front door?"

"Yes, are you going to let me in?"

"The door's unlocked, let yourself in—I can't walk…."

"What? Why? Oh, forget it, I'm coming in."

"Hiya, thanks for coming, I've…well er, I think I've…"

"What the hell are you doing sprawled on the floor? Oh my gosh, Chelsea, your foot! What've you done?"

"Dunno. Think it's broken. It's gone purple, and it hurts like hell. It's knocking me sick."

"I'm not surprised. It's swollen to twice the size of your other foot. You have phoned for an ambulance, haven't you?"

"No. I wanted to wait for you. I need you to help me."

"Seriously? I'm phoning straight away. Hang on, I'll make you a cup of tea while I'm doing it."

*****

"Tea, two sugars. Here you are."

"Thanks, Hun, I need this."

"They said the ambulance would be about ten minutes. While we wait, do you wanna tell me how you managed to break your ankle in an empty hallway?"

"Er, well, I actually broke it getting out of bed. It's kinda embarrassing…"

"Go on…"

"I thought I saw a spider, jumped up, and kicked the bed leg—you can't believe the agony, Chlo—and it turned out it was only a hair bobble."

"You daft sod! So how come you've only just got up? It's nearly ten am, and what are you wearing?"

"Oh this? It's just my new silk negligee—do you like it?"

"What? I mean, why are you wearing a sexy nightie? You normally sleep in a baggy T-shirt…and are you wearing make-up?"

"Yeah, just a little and I've been up for ages."

"So let me get this straight—you got up, got spooked by a hair bobble, broke your foot, while in agony you texted me, got changed into a sexy little number, put on your make-up and dragged your purple balloon foot all the way to the front door instead of phoning for an ambulance?"

"Erm…yeah. It sounds worse when you say it like that. Anyway, I need your help. Can you grab my phone from the bedroom, please? I forgot it."

"Okay, got it. What now?"

"When the ambulance arrives, can you video me for a TikTok video? This should get a ton of likes…."

"Chelsea, you really are unbelievable!"

Notes from the author

Some stories in this anthology have been featured in anthologies and magazines over the years—as shown below. If you have enjoyed my stories, check out similar stories by the authors I'm proud to work with.

Time After Time: And Other Stories – an anthology created by author Tom Benson.

Includes: Murky Windows

https://tombensonauthor.com/time-after-time-and-other-stories/

Next Steps – an anthology created by author Tom Benson.

Includes: The Magic Box of Apples and Earworm

https://tombensonauthor.com/next-steps/

Depths of Darkness – a psychological horror anthology, created by authors from the Indie Author Support and Discussion group.

Includes: Dwelling in the Shadows

https://www.amazon.co.uk/Depths-Darkness-Melanie-P-Smith-ebook/dp/B07ZBM25HP/

You're Not Alone: An Indie Author Anthology, created by Ian D. Moore. It includes uplifting stories by authors from the Inie Author Support and Discussion Group.

Includes: Lilies for the Mantel

https://www.amazon.co.uk/Youre-Not-Alone-Author-Anthology-ebook/dp/B00Y5RCOOE/

Connections eMagazine, created by author, Melanie P. Smith.

Most of the stories produced were for a picture prompt section in the magazine. This online magazine features stories, articles, new releases, book promotions, and an annual Reader's Choice Book Awards.

Includes: The Ring, Red Lights, No Fairytale, The Pitch

https://melaniepsmith.com/emagazine/

Strong Women – an anthology by contributors to Mom's Favorite Reads magazine. It features stories by thirteen new and best-selling authors, and is available on Amazon.

Includes: Hollin Hey, The Cupcake Hustle

https://books2read.com/u/bwv7A0

Mom's Favorite Reads magazine – created by authors Hannah Howe, Rebecca Carter and Denise McCabe.

Most of my flash fiction stories were produced for the flash challenge, run by Flash Fiction author Allison Symes.

https://issuu.com/momsfavoritereads

About the Author

Sylva Fae is a married mum of three from Lancashire, England. She grew up in a rambling old farmhouse with an artistic family and an adopted bunch of dysfunctional animals. Her earliest memories are of bedtime stories snuggled up close to Mum to see the pictures. It was a magical time, those last special moments before dozing off to sleep would feed dreams of faraway lands and mystical beings.

Sylva spent twenty-plus years teaching literacy to adults with learning difficulties and disabilities, and now lives in Cheshire, juggling being a mum, writing children's stories and keeping up with the crazy antics of their naughty rabbits.

Sylva and her family own a small woodland and escape there at every possible opportunity. Adventures in their own enchanted woodland, hunting for fairies and stomping in puddles, originally inspired Sylva to write stories for her girls, when they were younger. Whether it's sat on a log at the campfire in her own woods, or pottering around the beautiful local countryside, Sylva now finds her story inspiration being out in nature.

Sylva published her first children's book Rainbow Monsters, in 2017. She has since published seventeen other children's picture books, three chapter books, four illustrated anthologies, and has several short stories published in other anthologies. She also has a ridiculous number of books in her 'Work in Progress' folder.

Three of her books have won Best in Category for children's books at the Chanticleer International Book Awards and she's won seven Reader's Choice Awards. In addition to writing her own books, Sylva has ghost written several books, and is an editor and writer for Connections eMagazine.

Links

Amazon	author.to/SylvaFae
Facebook	https://www.facebook.com/SylvaFae
TikTok	@sylvafae54
Instagram	@sylvafae

And finally…

If you've enjoyed No Fairytale, please leave a short review on Amazon, and I promise not to kill you off in my next short story.

An annoying author quirk!

I finished this book with 55,455 words, and I was quite satisfied with this number. I do have a quirky love of numbers though, especially repetitive numbers and palindromic numbers, just like the character, Moira in 'Murky Windows'. Some numbers are just more pleasing than others! The number five is a particular favourite, though you may have guessed this from the repetition of fives in the stories. My fabulous author friend, Rebecca Bryn, suggested I add more words to make the total word count a super-satisfying 55,555. So, here are the extra words.

Printed in Great Britain
by Amazon